JUNE GEMINI

A NOVEL

WRITTEN & ILLUSTRATED BY

KOFA

This is a work of fiction. Names, characters, places, and incidents are the product of the author's imagination or used fictitiously.

JUNE GEMINI
Book 1
www.junegemini.com

Cover art and interior illustrations designed by Kofa.

ISBN: 0692852808
ISBN-13: 978-0692852804

To everyone that believed, thank you.

Especially mom.

ACKNOWLEDGMENTS

Carlton Jordan, the best coffee shop comrade
you could ever ask for. Chelsea Sonksen, for the
concise and gentle corrections. Jennifer Wang,
for knowing I could do better, and
Daniel Gradin, for the book that would inspire this.

Balance, must be maintained.

—THE CREATOR

1

A Doctor's Visit

"It has been a difficult few weeks as these bizarre disasters continue. And to add to the tragedy here, none of the families have been able to hold funerals for their loved ones, as the bodies have yet to be recovered. Reporting live from Manhattan Beach, California. This is Chris Mann, CNN."

The news broadcast entertained an empty living room in the Brooklyn home of Ahnie Abena. The sun had just started to settle, streaming light through the apartment's east-facing windows. Ahnie sat on the windowsill near the front door reading the Good Book, turning the delicate pages with care. The ringing sound of a timer at its expiration interrupted her read, prompting her to leave her cosy spot.

She placed the book into its engraved leather sleeve, put on her slippers and headed towards the kitchen. But something stopped her dead in her tracks. She crept along the cherry wood floor and reached across the dining table for a magazine, rolling it in half. Ahnie was focused as she stepped forward, raising the magazine above her head.

"Gotcha!" she yelled, swatting a spider dangling from the kitchen window. To her surprise, the magazine showed no sign of what should have been the remains of the arachnid. She spun around, holding the magazine in a ninja stance, scanning the area.

"Where are you, you little..."

A sudden knock at the front door startled her, causing the digest to drop. She held her chest and giggled, shaking her head in embarrassment.

A black town car she had never seen before was parked out front. Standing next to it was a clean-cut man in a suit wearing dark shades. There was another knock. *Better not be those Jehovah's Witness people*, she thought. She didn't recognize the face as she peered through the peephole. But she wasn't going to be rude, even in this neighborhood. She gracefully opened the door but kept the chain attached.

"Mrs. Abena?" asked the stranger.

"Miss," she sharply replied.

"My apologies, I'm Dr. Charles Risk. Sorry to disturb you this evening but I'd like to discuss your son's... health. Is he home?"

"His health?" she replied with a scowl. "He's fine."

"Umm, yes. I know. I mean... I'm sorry."

He fumbled for a moment, trying to find his words.

"Would you mind if I come in for a bit? I know this is strange… but your son is very sick."

"Where did you say you were from Doctor?" she asked.

He paused for a moment and remembered his manners.

"Ah, yes, of course," he said.

Charles reached into his vintage leather briefcase and pulled out a silver rectangular object. The shimmer it gave off made Ahnie reposition herself, carefully keeping an eye on what he was doing.

His hands squeezed the side of the object, propping it open. Inside was a small stack of cards. He slid one up and handed it to her.

"I'm from CURE," he proudly stated.

It was a brilliant white card, almost reflective. The front read: *Charles E. Risk*. Below it in a bold serif font read: CURE. But there was no address or phone number.

She glanced at the card, then back at him, then at the card, then back at him again. He was wearing a dark grey suit that was definitely tailored. Her time working at a local cleaner during her college years gave her an eye for that. But his shoes seemed too big and clunky for his size and height.

"Miss Abena, are you aware of the events that have occurred recently around the world?"

"Of course," she snapped. "It's all that's on the news. It's all everyone talks about."

"Well, CURE was the first to offer relief to those affected by the disasters," Charles said. "We're also leading the research to determine what caused them and whether they'll be happening again."

"I hear people saying it's the end of days," she added. "All these things keep happening and they just don't make sense."

"Like that one place in New Jersey where half a building just floats in the air. Is that real?"

Charles laughed, neither dismissing nor verifying her question.

"I assure you Miss Abena, the Earth will be around for a long time. Nothing to be overly alarmed about. I can personally guarantee that."

Ahnie adjusted her position at the door, leaning toward Charles to make sure he caught all of her sass.

"Overly alarmed? You don't think hundreds of people dying in a blink of an eye is something we should be alarmed about?"

"Of course, I meant, scientifically speaking…"

"You people always have a scientific explanation for everything. But sometimes things just can't be explained Doctor. Sometimes, it's just God's hand. Trust in the LORD with all your heart. And do not lean on your own understanding."

"Proverbs 3:5," Charles said.

Ahnie stood back, impressed. It wasn't everyday a well-dressed white man claiming to be a doctor knocks on her door *and* knows his scripture. She took another look at the card and glanced at him, squinting hard, as though that would make him give up his sham. He reached down to tuck the business card holder back into his bag. Before he could look back up, he heard the door shut.

Charles stood there for a moment, embarrassingly adjusting his jacket. He raised his hand again, about to knock when he heard the sound of chains rustling on the other side of the door.

"How do you like your coffee, Doctor?"

2

One Year Later

June gazed out the window as the sun began its descent above the Manhattan cityscape. The room had a minimal aesthetic and furnished only three objects: a bed, one long-stemmed plant, and a sixty-inch digital panel. The screen displayed a female reciting a calming ritual as holographic text extended beyond its surface. However, June's attention was fixated on the newsstand several stories below.

People hustled by, going about their busy lives. They moved swiftly on their way to do something that must have been very, very important. Most of them glared at the bright screens in their hands. It was as if this object was a map in a synchronized treasure hunt across the city.

A red-headed girl stood next to the stand, wearing a blue t-shirt that said KEEP CALM AND BE CUTE. Her mother wore the adult-sized version of the same t-shirt. She and a friend were chatting about how busy and tiring their lives were.

Even though he was several stories up, June could make out what they were saying. Or rather, what he wanted them to say. It was a game he played when he was bored. He mimicked them in his mind, chuckling to himself when their movements aligned with his improvisation.

Something about the way the mother held her daughter's hand made him think about the first time his dad took him into Manhattan. The large crowds and noisy ambience overwhelmed him as a child. But his father's firm grasp made him feel safe. He smiled as he admired the little girl. Her eyes were filled with the same wonder and fear that overtook him that day. He could almost hear his father's deep voice reassuring him as they plowed though the tireless sea of New Yorkers.

"Come June, we're almost there!"

Eventually they reached an opening with a newsstand on the corner. There was a tall, red cooler filled with assorted drinks and treats. His dad sensed his hesitation as they passed it.

"All right, go ahead and pick one. But it'll be our secret."

"OK!" June replied.

He was only allowed to have sweets once a day, and he already indulged in ice cream after breakfast.

Just out of his reach was what he wanted: a refreshingly sweet ice-cold Coca-Cola. He stretched out his six-year-old fingers, standing on his toes to grab the beverage.

Suddenly, the row of bottles were at eye level. His hands weren't that of a six year old anymore. He looked back to find that his father was also no longer there. A passerby bumped his shoulder spinning him around. In the reflection of the cooler's glass door he saw his current nineteen-year-old self. His feet felt the cold sting of the winter-kissed concrete. In shock, he dropped the glass bottle. It shattered on impact startling the little girl. Everyone's attention shifted toward the place the sound had originated. But when they looked, no one was there.

3

A Doctor's Visit: Part 2

"Coffee would be nice, thank you. And you can call me Charles," replied the doctor.

"Nice to meet you Charles. That's a wonderful name," Ahnie said. "And you can call me Ahnie."

"Annie is a pleasant name as well," Charles said.

Ahnie laughed. "You people have a way of pronouncing things. It's Ahh-knee."

"My apologies, Ahh-knee."

"Forgiven. Your coffee?"

"Actually, my wife doesn't like me eating things too sweet. If she were here she'd only let me add a little bit of cream," Charles said.

It wasn't true, but it allowed him to suggest he had a wife. He hoped it would make Ahnie more comfortable.

"I promise not to tell," Ahnie replied.

"Well, then throw in a bit of sugar if it's not too much trouble."

"None at all."

A few seconds later, Charles heard the sound of clanking mugs and running water. It meant Ahnie was preoccupied which gave him the opportunity to observe every detail in the room.

It was a traditional single-family townhouse, much smaller than his current living quarters but the same size as the home he grew up in.

The abundance of pictures throughout the space caught his attention. Particularly the ones of a boy, captured at different ages. Most were either of the boy by himself or with his mother. One photo next to the television showed a man dressed in a military uniform with the words Semper Fi around the frame.

Ahnie returned with two mugs of steaming coffee.

"One fresh cup," she politely stated, handing him the mug.

Charles took a sip almost immediately.

"Mm that's good, really good. It has a spicy yet sweet flavor that I've never experienced before. May I ask where I can find such delicious coffee?"

Again, Ahnie seemed impressed.

"You have an exquisite palette Charles. That is Limu coffee from southwest Ethiopia."

He took another careful sip.

"So, your husband is in the military?"

"Not married, remember?"

"Ah yes, forgive me. It's been a long day."

"It's barely six o'clock," Ahnie said. "But I know doctors are on call twenty-four seven."

"Actually I just flew in from Japan. We're... expanding. Landed at JFK about an hour ago."

"Okay..." Ahnie said.

She repositioned herself in the love seat across from him. Charles interpreted it as her being uncomfortable.

"Why don't you tell me why you think my son is sick?" she asked.

Charles grinned.

"I don't think you would have let me in if you didn't have some idea of what I was talking about."

Ahnie didn't respond. She took a careful sip from her mug. Her sharp eyes did the talking.

"Let me ask you something Ahnie. Have you noticed your son exhibiting any strange behavior? Anything you might not be able to understand? Or even explain?"

She took another sip.

"Why don't we start by you telling me why you are here. It was you that came knocking on my door," she reminded him.

"Fair enough," replied the doctor. But before I begin, I have to ask that whatever we discuss remain strictly confidential."

"Of course," she blinked.

"Perfect."

He took a sip of his coffee.

"This is really good. I'll have to track down some for the office."

Ahnie cleared her throat to signal her impatience. Charles opened his briefcase and pulled out several photos. One was of a young Asian girl, about thirteen years old. Her eyes were large for her head and she had the most innocent-looking smile. The other photos were of a school that appeared to have suffered tremendous structural damage. The entire building was leveled. Papers were flying about, broken glass and dried blood littered the scene. Ahnie jumped back when she noticed a severed leg among the rubble.

"Sorry, I should have warned that the photos may be a bit graphic," Charles said. "Take a look at this young girl. What do you think of her?"

A look of horror took over Ahnie's face as she covered her mouth.

"Oh no, don't tell me she…"

"Her name is Miko. She is alive and well."

A sigh of relief washed over Ahnie.

Charles showed her more photos of the destruction. These were interior shots of the rubble. The classrooms, or what remained of them were covered in blood and human remains.

"What a tragedy. But… I don't understand how my son being sick has to do with this," Ahnie asked. She leaned back, crossing her arms. "This isn't making any sense."

"Ahnie, the girl in the photo is the one *responsible* for what you just saw."

He pulled out another picture of Miko. It was a portrait-like mug shot except there were no height measurements behind her. Just a white wall.

"I'm not following," she replied.

He handed the picture to Ahnie.

"Take a close look at her eyes. Do they look familiar to you?"

Ahnie took a careful look at the photo, struggling to see what the doctor was trying to show her. Charles noticed this and placed another picture of Miko in front of her.

"This is what her eyes look like now," Charles said, pointing at the first portrait. "But her birth certificate says she was born with brown eyes," he said, tapping Miko's official school headshot. He reached into his wallet and pulled out another photo. It was a casual family snapshot.

"This is my wife, Elizabeth."

Ahnie looked at the image and forced a smile.

"She's very pretty."

"We've been married for twenty years. I can describe every detail from the first time we met. She was a country girl working as a nurse at a local clinic. While on a business trip, I had a golfing accident that needed immediate attention. When I walked into the clinic, her striking eyes made me completely forget why I was there. They were blue. They were blue back then."

He paused to collect himself.

"And now, she's very ill. Would you mind looking at her eyes in this picture Ahnie?"

He showed her another picture of Elizabeth in a hospital bed. Her skin was almost as white as the sheets and room that enclosed her. In the photo her eyes were green.

Charles pointed at a picture on the wall of a teenage boy with a track medal around his neck.

"I noticed your son's eyes are brown in all of his photos. If I may ask, what color are they now?"

Ahnie placed her hand on her forehead and took a deep breath. She reached for her purse and pulled out her cellphone. After several swipes, she paused and clutched the phone tightly to her chest.

4

CURE

June was madly screaming. His body contorted as two nurses held him down while a third prepared an injection. A group of kids dressed in white peeked into the room through the glass window. The scene wasn't uncommon or unusual but it provided a level of excitement that didn't come very often.

"Hold him down!"

"Preparing the serum, ten seconds to injection!"

Among the spectators in the hall was Novelle. Her beautiful face and curly hair always stood out from the crowd. Her exposed mid section distracted the boys as she stretched to look through the translucent pane. She pulled down her top when she felt their eyes on her.

"Tsss, ya boy's an idiot," said Terrence, the biggest and most macho of the group. "He must be pushing it too far. Dummy."

Novelle rolled her eyes—her usual response to anything Terrence said.

June continued to yell out from excruciating pain.

"How much longer?" asked James, one of the nurses.

He was a muscular black guy in his mid-forties with a shiny bald head. Along his arms were tattoos that suggested he'd been to prison. The other two nurses were Jon and Victoria. Jon was thirty-something—a white guy with a military cut. His physique wasn't as impressive as James' but he was slightly taller. Victoria, the veteran of the three, was Vietnamese. Her straight black hair was usually in a bun. Depending on her style and make-up for the day, her perceived age fluctuated between twenty-one and forty.

"Prepare for injection!" Victoria instructed.

She was holding a long syringe filled with a purplish liquid. Jon restrained June's upper body while James, the strongest of the three, held down his legs.

Victoria injected the serum into June's right arm and he began to calm almost immediately. His arms were still fighting the restraints but his legs had gone limp. It caught Victoria's attention.

"We need a chair."

Victoria said this as she looked back at the curious eyes peeping through the glass. Everyone scattered, except for Novelle.

"Damn this kid's strong as shit!" James exerted. "I didn't know that was one of the things they could do."

Victoria positioned her stethoscope to check June's heart rate. "Jon, see what's up with that chair."

"But he's the new guy," Jon snapped.

Victoria narrowed her eyes at him above her spectacles.

"Ok, no problem," Jon agreed.

He purposely bumped into James' shoulder on his way out.

"Da hell?" James responded.

"Still a kid," Victoria said while shaking her head.

She continued to check June's vitals, noting anything that seemed irregular. James was still in a state of shock but his training taught him how to play it cool.

"I thought this only happened the first time they do, you know, whatever it is that they can do."

"It can happen anytime they push too far," Victoria said. "But this one is different somehow. His tantrums seem more intense than the others."

She removed a pen-shaped object from her shirt pocket and clicked the button at the top. A small light emitted from the tip. June was now completely calm and breathing normally but he was unconscious. She lifted his eyelid to check his pupils.

"They know the consequences of pushing too far yet they do it anyway. Sometimes they can't see for a couple days or they black out. Others experience hearing loss. Everyone's different."

She released June's eyelid and placed the pen back in her coat pocket.

"Maybe the pain is not as bad as we thought it was. Maybe they're just muscle spasms or something," James said.

Victoria took off her glasses. A lanyard kept them hanging around her neck.

"Did you ever play with matches as a kid, Mr. Cooper?"

James was caught off-guard by the question. He heard from the staff that when Victoria addressed you by your last name it meant you were in trouble.

"The tip of a match, when lit, can get as hot as seven hundred degrees. Did you know that James?"

He exhaled a sense of relief.

"Imagine taking a needle and holding it to a flame for about two minutes or so. Of course you may not be able to hold onto it for that long but let's say you did… until the needle was as hot as the head of that match."

She lifted her right index finger to illustrate her point.

"Then, while the needle is hot…"

She swiftly grabbed his left wrist, depressing her thumb into his veins.

"Let's say I take that needle, starting at the tip of your middle finger, and push it directly into the median nerve. It continues through your forearm traveling all the way up to your shoulder. Right before it makes its way into your chest, it splits into fragments, traveling through your entire body, all the way down your legs, down to your toes."

She pinched his wrist as she said this, then let go.

"Our scans show hyper-activity in the dorsal posterior insula, the brain's pain center. It's something I wouldn't wish on anyone, even my ex-mother-in-law."

"Damn," James said.

"The serum stops the pain and prevents further nerve damage. But like I said, each patient's response is different."

"So we're helping them, right?" James asked.

Victoria put her glasses back on and quickly grabbed her clipboard.

"You ask a lot of questions, Mr. Cooper. I'm gonna keep an eye on you."

Victoria left the room, walking past Novelle as if she wasn't there.

"Is June ok?" Novelle asked.

"He'll live," Victoria replied, without stopping or pulling her attention away from her clipboard.

5

Novelle

She awoke calmly, revealing striking green eyes. The sun peeked though the gray sky as a sharp pain ran through her body. She raised her hand to block the light.

"What the?"

"Snow?" she mumbled, attempting to rise.

Her body responded with more pain.

She tried to move again but was only slightly more successful. She wallowed a few feet before her face and the snow found each other.

"Shit!"

Beneath the thin layer of snow was a coarse material that stuck to her face.

There was an uncomfortable tingle as she brushed it off and spat out a few grains.

"Hate sand."

Faint screams and mechanical noise echo around her. They gradually gained volume as she stumbled along the beach. She closed her eyes, trying to make out a voice within the noise. As her mind settled, the words started to take form.

"Help! Please, somebody! Help us!"

The howl seemed to come from behind mounds of sand lining the beach. She climbed the berm using her hands for support. Flurries and strong winds pushed her about as she reached the top. *Why the hell is snow here*, she thought.

Directly on the other side was a heavy-set black woman crouching over a teenage boy. The gold and purple hue of his jersey shimmered as she approached them.

"Praise God! Thank you, Jesus. He done sent an angel," the woman celebrated.

The boy had a metal shard stuck in the side of his abdomen. The jersey was tainted red from blood. His eyes were open, but he was having difficulty breathing. He coughed up more blood as Novelle knelt down to take a look at the wound. The cold sensation of the slush and sand soiled her knees as she examined him. She pressed slightly above the deadly fragment to see how deep it penetrated him.

"He's gonna be fine, but we need to stop the bleeding," Novelle said. "You see where my hand is?"

"Yes," the woman responded.

"I need you to apply pressure here. I'm gonna go find some help."

As she released her hand from the wounded area, the boy grabbed Novelle, and their eyes met.

He tried to speak, lifting his head, but couldn't utter the words. After a moment he let her go.

The fog seemed to be clearing up, allowing Novelle to make out a lifeguard tower in the distance. She guided the woman's hand to the boy's wound.

"Keep the pressure constant, right here. There has to be a first aid kit in the tower. I'll be right back."

The woman reluctantly did as she was instructed.

"I'm Rose. And this is my son Michael," she said.

Novelle locked eyes with the boy again, and looked back at the mother.

"Novelle. My name's Novelle."

"God bless you sweetheart. Thank you."

Novelle nodded.

She found strength as she ran along the beach, knowing her actions could effect the outcome of the boy. The fog gave way, exposing the chaos.

People were scattered about, many of them lying motionless. All of them covered with dirt and soot, as if they spent the day coal mining. The loud cries of a toddler with blonde hair and colorful trunks caught her attention.

"Mom-meeeee!"

"Mom-meee!" yelled the tot.

"Hey, are you lost?" Novelle asked as she knelt down to his level. The kid continued to wail. She looked around and saw that no one seemed to be looking for the boy.

"Ok, you're coming with me."

She picked him up, carrying him as she headed toward the tower. The beach was riddled with metal debris and injured people. Novelle looked out into the ocean and saw the source of the madness: the remains of a commercial aircraft bobbing in the water.

"Oh my God!"

She stood there frozen, questioning if what she saw was real. The youngster's cry brought her back.

A few bodies were floating near the plane. Several others were swimming toward shore. A middle-aged man was approaching them, and Novelle could see that he was struggling.

"Stay right here, ok?"

She placed the toddler down and removed her hooded college sweatshirt.

She jumped in the water and swam toward the man. It didn't take her long to reach him. She wrapped her arm around his torso and assisted him to the shore.

"Thank you," he said breathlessly.

She nodded, panting from the swim.

Her eyes scanned the beach in panic. No sign of the kid, but a red and white jacket caught her attention.

"Thank God."

She was out of breath by the time she reached the lifeguard. He was giving CPR to a woman lying unconscious.

"Hey, there's a kid bleeding out badly back there..."

He threw her a can't-you-see-I'm-busy look.

"Supplies. In your tower?" she asked.

The Lifeguard was applying pressure to the woman's chest. He blew two breaths into her mouth then threw his head to the left.

"Second cabinet from the bottom. I'll come find you."

Novelle sprinted to the tower. It had already been ransacked, but there were loose bandages and miscellaneous items on the floor. She grabbed two bandages and a small tube of dressing.

As she walked out, she heard the toddler's cry from the other side of the tower. She scooped him up, balancing the supplies in her other hand.

"It's ok. It's ok. I got chu."

She should have been winded. But carrying the kid while dashing across the sand was easier than she'd anticipated. She assumed it was because of the adrenalin.

Rose's hands were still in the same position but now soaked in Michael's blood.

"I didn't know what to do. The bleeding... it won't stop," Rose cried.

Novelle sat the toddler down.

"Stay right here ok?" She ruffled his hair the same way she did with her kid sister and knelt next to Michael as she prepared the bandage.

"How are you doing?" she asked.

His eyes were closed and he wasn't responding. Novelle checked Michael's pulse then leaned her ear against his chest.

"Come on Michael. Stay with us."

Novelle placed a hand on his abdomen for support while she slowly pulled out the shard. She tore apart the package of bandages with her teeth and administered dressing to the wounded area, as she was shown just a few weeks earlier.

She checked his pulse again.

"We're losing him."

She clasped her hands and began applying pressure to his chest.

"Come on... breathe for me."

"Breathe..."

"One, two, three, four... come on buddy... one, two, three, four."

She leaned back, looked to the sky, and let out a deep breath.

"Come on, come on, come on…"

She blew air into his mouth and listened for a heartbeat.

"One, two, three, four… Come on! … COME ON! Stay with me Michael…"

His mother gently placed her hand on Novelle's shoulder as she attempted another round of thrusts.

"It's okay, baby," she said.

Novelle's chest was heaving dramatically.

"It's okay… it's okay…"

Tears fell from Rose's eyes as she held the toddler tight, turning him away so he couldn't see Michael.

Novelle continued to push at Michael's chest.

"One, two, three, four…"

A rush of pain and anger shot through her body as she tried to resuscitate him.

"No…"

She looked toward the sky and let out another breath. Around her, the scene had grown increasingly chaotic. She peeled back the bandage to examine the wound.

"The bleeding stopped…"

She began thrusting at Michael's chest again, counting with each movement.

"One, two, three, four… Come on! One, two, three, four… Come on, Michael…"

She swung her right hand back, making a fist and swung it down onto Michael's chest.

"COME-ON!"

Michael's head and chest suddenly jerked. He turned sideways, coughing loudly.

Novelle fell on her left side, exhausted, and felt a tingle of pain run through her body. She closed her eyes for a second. When she re-opened them, she made out two lifeguards approaching with a stretcher.

"Too-too-too-tooo…. Too-too-too-tooo."

The ringing was coming from beneath the sand. She sifted through and found a cellphone.

"Hello?"

"Hello?"

"I'm sorry, but there's… there's been a terrible accident."

She paused to listen.

"I'm sorry, but I haven't seen him. Yes, I know, I have his phone. But there's, there's been an accident. Ma'am… I would love to but I don't know how to…"

She pulled the phone away from her ear with a look of frustration and had a thought. She dialed a sequence of ten numbers and pressed connect. It rang several times and went to voicemail.

"Come on, somebody pick up."

She dialed the number again. It rang seven times, and again went to voicemail.

She exhaled and dialed a different number.

It rang five times.

"Hello?" answered a spritely young female.

"Luna, it's me. I need to talk to mom."

"Novelle? Novey! What's with the weird number? Did you lose your phone again?"

"Where's Mom? Put her on."

"Novey, can you believe it? It's snowing outside."

"Crazy right? I mean, snow around here? Uh… weird city. She's gonna be mad you lost your phone again. Did it get stolen on the train? I know they steal people's phones out there. You gotta be careful, Novey, especially on those trains," Luna rambled.

"Luna, Mom, now!" Novelle demanded.

Luna's response was muffled by static.

"Luna. Luna?"

"Novelle? Where are you?"

"Mom," Novelle tearfully responded. "I'm so happy to hear your voice."

"Are you o…"

"Mom, are you there?"

"There's… earth…"

"Mom, I can't understand."

A loud crash came from the other end of the phone, hurting Novelle's ears.

"Mom, what was that? Are you okay?"

"Luna? Mom? Please…" Novelle wept.

A deep, monstrous rumble that sounded like a thousand horses emitted from the ocean, followed by a light spray of water. Something seemed to be blocking the sun as a titanic shadow covered the beach. Novelle turned.

"Oh, my God," she said as the phone slipped from her fingertips.

A three-hundred-foot tidal wave towered above her.

6

June

"Watch. If she's on the A, I'm definitely getting the number," June said as he confidently rubbed his hands together.

"I'm from Missouri, so you gotta show me bruh," Jonas replied. He took a drag from his cigarette and exhaled smoothly before handing it to June. Jonas was taller than June but skinny compared to June's muscular physique. His long hair looked like he hadn't showered in weeks, but in a cool way. *As long as the ladies like it,* was his mantra.

June took a nervous drag from the cigarette and coughed twice.

"Rookie lungs," Jonas laughed as he took the cigarette back from June.

"I'm telling you, she was on me man," June said as he brushed the tip of his nose with his right thumb. "My swag was up that day, especially how your boy ran that four-hundred."

He pumped his knees, swinging his hands in a running motion.

"Something about the way she looked at me though. It was like… she knew me or something. And those eyes man… I'm telling you Jonas, she was bad. Michael Jackson bad."

"Man how you know she feelin' you when you ain't even talk to the broad?" Jonas chuckled. "She probably thought you were just another weird dude on the train. And you almost lost that last race playing too much. I be see-in' you. Going all out from the jump. Doing the most."

"Yeah whateva man," June replied. "Let's just catch this train before we miss first period."

Jonas took another drag of the cigarette, exhaled, and flicked it into the street.

"Man how many times we gonna ride this train hoping to see this one chick? It's been what, two months now? Maybe she changed her routine after she realized she had a stalker on the A!"

June shook his head playfully in disagreement.

"I'm telling you Jonas. She's dope man, trust. Just the way she looked back at me when she got off the train…" June said as he tapped his heart repeatedly.

"She had this curly reddish-dark hair that was crazy dope too. Never saw anybody like that before. Except in a magazine or TV or something. And her eyes…

They were bright green like she was Mother Nature or something. I'm telling you she was on some other shit."

"You really about this one huh?" Jonas said as he tapped his front and back pockets. "Aww shit! Can you spot me? I left my Metro in my other pants."

"Got chu," June responded.

"My dude."

They barely caught the next train. The usual commuters were all in attendance. Businessmen and women in corporate attire who wore sneakers during their commute, service workers, bums and tourists—people from different walks of life.

The school bell rang in room 307. Four minutes later, June and Jonas arrived as Mrs. Coleman completed roll call.

"Nice of you gentlemen to make it in today," she said as they scrambled to their seats.

"Aww sorry Mrs. C," Jonas said. "June fell in love on the train again."

The whole class erupted in laughter.

"Ok everyone settle down."

"And thank you for disrupting homeroom as usual Mr. Florence," Mrs. Coleman remarked.

"You know I just be trying to make you laugh Mrs. C," responded Jonas with a grin. A collective "ooooooh" came from the class. It made Mrs. Coleman blush.

"Ok settle down folks. I hope you all studied well for the test."

Grumbles came from around the room. Jonas looked back towards June with a surprised but disappointed look on his face. As he turned forward, a crumbled piece of paper struck his head and landed at his feet. Without turning, he stuck his middle finger at June behind his head.

"You guys had ample time to prepare and I offered to tutor anyone after class who needed additional help. Clear your desks. Phones in the basket you know the drill. When you're finished you get your phone back."

One at a time the students walked to the front of the room and placed their cellphones in the 'holding cell' as they called it. After they released their devices, Mrs. Coleman passed the tests down each row.

"You have thirty-five minutes to complete the exam. Keep your papers faced down until everyone has their test."

The students settled into their seats and waited for the long hand to hit twelve. Mrs. Coleman looked at her watch and then at the clock on the wall. Nervous coughs and clearing of throats came from around the room.

"Ok and… go!"

Jonas nervously rubbed his head in frustration. It was cool in the classroom but a bead of sweat ran down the side of his neck. He looked to the right and to the left. Everyone had their heads down, focused on the test.

"Pssst…pssst…" June signaled to him.

Jonas turned back and June stretched his eyes wide while looking at the floor next to Jonas. Right beside the foot of the chair was the crumpled paper June threw at him. Jonas looked up to check on what Mrs. Coleman was doing. She was buried in of her romance novels.

Keeping his eyes on Mrs. Coleman, Jonas used his left leg to drag the ball of paper closer. He pulled it close enough that he could pick it up. Then he slid his pen off the edge of the desk. It hit the floor making the loudest noise possible. No one else noticed. He reached down, grabbed the pen, and scooped up the paper all in one swoop. He carefully uncurled it, trying not to make a sound. When he had it almost flat, he slid it under his test and looked up to see that Mrs. Coleman's book still had her full attention. Jonas slid the test up, revealing the straightened rough paper underneath.

"My dude," he said under his breath.

He looked back at June and gave him a nod. When he turned back to his test, Mrs. Coleman was standing right over him.

"What is that Mr. Florence?" she asked.

"What you mean?" Jonas replied.

"This!" she stated, lifting up the test to reveal the rough sheet underneath. June face-palmed and shook his head.

"Both of you. Hallway. Now!"

A collective "ooooooh" came from the class.

Jonas and June stood in the hallway with their backs against the wall. Mrs. Coleman entered with two slips of paper in her hand.

"Jonas, take this to the Dean's office," she instructed.

"Aww Mrs. Coleman, I had nothing to do with this," Jonas said. "I didn't even know what it was. I had no idea June wrote the answers on that paper."

"What? Really Jonas?" June said.

"Mrs. Coleman I swear to you. I ain't have nothing to do with this. I studied last night I don't need no cheat sheet," Jonas said.

"And you'll have the opportunity to prove it," she sternly replied.

Jonas took the slip and headed down the hall, avoiding eye contact with his friend. When he cleared the corner Mrs. Coleman turned to June.

"As for you, what were you thinking? You know how strongly I dislike cheating in my class."

June couldn't make eye contact with her.

"I was just trying to look out Mrs. C. You know," June said.

"Look out? Mrs. C? That's not June talking."

She looked down the hall to see if anyone else was around.

"Why are you acting like these damn hoodlums from the street?" she whispered. "That is not you. I know you didn't need to cheat but it's just as bad trying to help someone do it."

She stepped in closer to June and lifted his chin up.

"I had a good talk with your mother at the parent teacher conference. What's going on with you?"

June didn't respond.

"Come on June, tell me something. Or I may have to send you to the Dean. And I know Coach Anderson won't like that."

June looked at his feet.

"Oh don't tell me you're one of those," she added.

"One of those?" June scoffed.

"One of those... I - hate - the - world - cause - my - father -ain't - around."

"The hell you say?" June snapped. "What you know about me? Or my father?" he said aggressively beating his chest.

Mrs. Coleman backed off, nervously bumping into the door behind her.

"You think cause you're married to a black man it gives you the goddamn right to talk to me like that?"

Mrs. Coleman jiggled the doorknob to the classroom and slid inside, locking the door behind her. Moments later, two uniformed security guards approached June in the hallway.

"Oh, you called security on me?"

"Just take it easy," one of the guards said as he grabbed June's arm.

"Get your damn hands off me bro. I didn't do anything!"

Students huddled near the classroom doors watching the incident through the glass opening.

"Just take it easy buddy…" the other guard said as they attempted to restrain him. June resisted, prompting the guards to apply force. The larger of the two tried to pull June's arms behind him. They tussled until June was pinned to the floor.

"This is bullshit man!" June yelled. "I didn't do anything man! I didn't do anything!"

They handcuffed him and yanked him to his feet.

"I didn't do anything! This is bullshit!" he continued as they took him away.

After a firm conversation with Mrs. Coleman, Ahnie signed paperwork and escorted June to the car. They drove for several minutes in silence.

"So you cheat on tests and disrespect teachers now?" Ahnie asked.

She looked over as June scrolled through his cell phone, reviewing texts from people asking what happened. A notification popped up on the top that read: *Jonas: My fault bro.*

June tapped the entry field to respond, but hesitated. Instead he pressed the power button and reached over to turn on the radio. An obnoxious rap song was playing. Ahnie quickly turned it off. June turned and slumped his head toward the passenger window. They drove for a few blocks when a father running after his son caught his attention. The dad caught the little boy, picked him up, and hugged him close.

"So you got nothing to say?" his mother asked.

June didn't respond.

"And put your seatbelt on. How many times do I have to tell you?"

June buckled his seatbelt with the enthusiasm of a wet towel.

"I didn't cheat on no damn test," he mumbled.

"Who do you think you're talking to? This is the second time this month I had to leave work early to pick you up from school. Explain yourself!"

She grabbed his face and turned it toward her.

"And watch your tone."

"You didn't even remember," June said.

Ahnie shook her head and exhaled. The car was quiet for the next three minutes.

"You think I don't know what this week is? I explained that to Mrs. Coleman. Which is why she agreed you can take the test tomorrow after school. And no detention so you can still practice with the team. But with one condition."

"What?"

His mother gave him a serious look.

"I mean, what's the catch?" he asked.

"All you have to do is apologize."

"Why should I have to apologize? I didn't do anything! She didn't have the right," he sniffed. "She didn't have the right."

June turned his head toward the window to hide the tears streaming down his face. They came to a stop sign. Ahnie reached over and softly grabbed his face, turning it toward her again.

"I miss him too."

She rubbed his chin then reached behind him and lovingly stroked the back of his neck.

"I know your father's passing would be hard on you this week. But you have to remember, I love you too. And baby, God doesn't give us anything we cannot handle."

She smiled, looking deep into his eyes.

"You are strong, smart, and you care a lot about people. Sometimes even more than you care for yourself. I understand you were trying to help your friend, so I'm not upset with you for that. But…"

Ahnie proceeded through the intersection.

"That temper of yours. God knows. When you were born, we knew you'd be a feisty one," she laughed.

June tried to stay angry but a slight grin forced it's way through. He shook his head then turned to face his mother. Her smile was as radiant as ever.

Something approaching their car through her window caught his attention. His eyes stretched wide open as he panicked.

"Mom!" June yelled as he raised his palm toward the driver's side window.

A delivery truck was a split second away from slamming into Ahnie's side of the car. But instead of feeling the impact that would have surely killed them, they saw the truck hover in mid-air, an inch from Ahnie's window—with its tires spinning wildly.

7

A Doctor's Visit: Part 3

"We're reporting to you live from Manhattan Beach California. It's a beach city just south of Los Angeles International Airport. Known for its summer volleyball tournaments and prolific surfing community, it is the epitome of southern Californian living."

"Residents describe what appears to be a colossal tidal wave that recently struck the city. This is unlike anything ever seen in this region. I'm currently standing at the corner of Highland Avenue and Manhattan Boulevard. This is the closest we can get to the beach, without stepping into the water."

"If you notice the palm trees behind me… a few weeks ago, you would have been able to walk past them and down to the pier. But as you can see, that area is now totally submerged. The event has claimed the lives of over two hundred people. Among them were passengers of a downed plane approaching LAX. It has taken local and federal authorities several weeks just to clear out the area. But as you can see, there is still a lot of damage."

"With us now is David. David has been a resident of Manhattan Beach for over fifteen years, and a witness of the event. David, can you describe what you saw?"

"Yeah, um, yeah. It was unbelievable. I walk my dog Lefty here along the beach almost every day. And uh, that morning me and Lefty head out and I see parts of a plane just floating in the water with smoke coming out of it. You could see people swimming away from it and stuff. I wanted to go down and help, but Lefty wouldn't go out to the beach. I was like, 'Lefty what are you doing?' Then out of nowhere, it started snowing."

"Snowing?" responded the puzzled reporter.

"Yeah, snow. Crazy. It started coming down, and I was like what the hell? I was about to call 911 but realized I left my phone at home. So I head home, get my phone, and when I get back, I see this giant wave coming at the pier. First I thought something was wrong with my eyes cause I didn't have my contacts in, or that I was going crazy or something."

David paused for a moment, turning slightly.

"I'm sorry, do you mind stopping the camera?" he asked.

The reporter seemed confused, shifting his position while looking at the cameraman.

"Is everything okay, David?"

David placed his face into his palm as he seemed to tear up.

"I'm just so grateful for this little guy. If it weren't for Lefty... I wouldn't even be here. I would have been a goner. But those poor people on the beach didn't have a chance. Even the ones that ran in to help them. All of them, gone. And it happened right in front of me. Like it was nothing. Like it was in a movie or something."

The reporter gently placed his hand on David's shoulder and gave him two slights pats.

"And what did you feel in that moment?" he asked.

"I felt... I felt a rumble. It felt like an earthquake when the wave hit the pier. People were screaming. Some tried to run. But it came so fast."

"Been here fifteen years... never seen anything like that. I just don't know. Stuff like this never happens around here."

"Thank you David," interrupted the reporter.

He turned to face the camera and deliver his closing statement.

"It has been a difficult few weeks as coverage of these bizarre natural disasters continue."

"Nothing natural about that..." mumbled David.

The reporter pinched his lips and bowed his head in sorrow.

"And to add to the tragedy here, none of the families have been able to hold funerals for their loved ones, as the bodies have yet to be recovered. Reporting live from Manhattan Beach, California. This is Chris Mann, CNN."

Ahnie held the phone close to her chest, with her back facing the doctor.

"I wasn't sure if it was an act of God or if I was imagining the whole thing," Ahnie said.

She exhaled deeply, looking up at the ceiling.

"All I know is that truck should have killed us. It was so close I could smell the heat from its tires. I could smell the motor oil," Ahnie said.

She turned to face Charles.

"It stopped dead in its tracks, right outside my door. We should have been hit. We should have been dead. But there we were. Still alive."

"So, what do you think happened?" Charles asked.

"The truck was frozen, like it was suspended in time. Didn't make any sense. I knew it had to be God. For whatever reason, it wasn't our time. And when God has a plan for you, nothing stands in the way of that."

She looked again at the phone, then back at Charles.

"What happened after that?" Charles asked.

"Everything started to shake. It took a while to realize what was going on. Telephone poles fell and people were running around crazy. I couldn't believe what was happening. I never experienced one before so I wasn't sure what it was."

"You mean the earthquake?" Charles asked.

"Yes, but something happened with June. He went into a seizure—his arms and legs were all over the place. I could tell something was hurting him and it was very painful. It all came so fast. Next thing I knew I was waking up in the hospital."

Dr. Risk pulled out a tablet and wrote something down.

"And what did they tell you?"

"That's the thing. They told me the earthquake had caused our accident. I felt fine, but June was unconscious for a few hours. They revived him and suggested he stay a few days for testing. After about a week, they let me bring him home. I was happy to have him back, but I could tell something was off. Something was different about him."

She handed Charles her cell phone. It was a picture of her and June when she picked him up from the hospital. The doctor slid his fingers over the screen to zoom in on the photo. June's eyes were green.

8

CURE: Part 2

"Choose…"

A faceless man dressed in white spoke the words that echoed around June.

"You must choose," whispered the ominous voice.

There were no walls in the infinite white space. The voice came from all directions—even though the man stood directly behind him. But whenever June turned around, somehow the man would still be in the same position.

June stood still, examining his hands. His translucent skin exposed a stream of energy. It felt like warm beads of water trickling through his arm.

The energy shifted into a sticky, black matter and began pouring from June's mouth and eyes. He found himself swimming in a sea of it. Bodies of ivory-skinned beings emerged from beneath the matter, attempting to pull him under. They had no facial features, just a patch of skin where their eyes, nose, and mouth should have been. The stronger he fought against them, the more aggressive they became. Slowly, the matter pulled him in, until all was dark. He swung his arms about, trying to thwart them off but noticed there was no longer any resistance. He was fighting thin air.

At his feet a sea of skulls and bones flowed by. In the distance, a faint silhouette of a city under fire.

A butterfly fluttered ahead of him, out of focus, about ten yards away. As his eyes adjusted to see it, the butterfly mysteriously traveled the distance between them, and was now perched on the tip of his index finger. He delicately pulled his hand closer to examine the insect, but it disintegrated into a gust of sand.

The sky opened, revealing the depths of outer space. It felt as close as the top roof of a three-story building. Through the opening he could see the stars stream by, and he felt the inertia of the earth's rotation. The sound of traffic emanated from behind. He turned to investigate and somehow he was now in the middle of Times Square. A loud crackling sound caught his attention as a comet flew by. He realized the stars were passing less frequently, and he felt the earth's rotation come to a standstill. His entire world decelerated until everything around him was in a mannequin state.

There was a deep rumble in the distance, followed by a dark cloud of scattered debris. The dark mass approached June, engulfing everything and everyone around him.

All structures and flesh dissipated to dust, adding to the dark mass. As it passed, everything was wiped clean, bringing June back to the original white space.

"You must choose," said the celestial voice.

June quickly pivoted, but again the entity was behind him. Suddenly, a blinding light overtook the space and when it subsided, June found himself in his bed, comfortable, with the sheets neatly tucked over him. He attempted to swing out of the bed, but his legs wouldn't respond.

"Damn."

Using his left arm, he pushed his body upright, switching to his right arm for balance. At the bottom of the bed was a wheelchair. It might as well have been a mile away. Again, he tried to stand, but his legs collapsed like freshly cooked pasta. He didn't have to use them, he thought. He could bring the chair to him. But the athlete in him saw everything as a challenge, and he didn't want the easy way out.

Since the day he realized what he could do, he didn't *have* to touch a door ever again—except in the presence of others.

As he rolled down the hall, a group of kids ranging from twelve to sixteen, all dressed in the same white attire, nearly ran him over.

"Sorry June!" Miko said.

She was the youngest of all the patients in the facility. Her eyes were green, like his. Like every other one of them.

The announcement over the intercom reminded everyone that lunch was being served in the main cafeteria, which sent the kids running back past him.

"Sorry June!" Miko repeated as she playfully whisked by.

He felt a jolt on the back of his chair as his speed suddenly increased.

"Look who decided to leave his room for once," Terrence announced.

He was running at full speed, with June's wheelchair in front of him.

"Quit playing, T! What the hell?" June said.

Terrence's evil grin widened as he ran with the wheelchair. His laugh was both goofy and sinister.

"Shoulda' thought of that before you…"

He stopped mid-sentence when he saw Victoria at the end of the hall. It was strange he noticed her first. Her uncanny attentiveness was replaced with a zombie-like state as she flipped through the small stack of paperwork on her clipboard. He threw her a smile as he casually wheeled June past her. June knew she saw them, but for whatever reason she didn't acknowledge them. Victoria stepped in one of the four elevators and entered a seven-digit sequence on the digital keypad.

As soon as the doors shut, June and Terrence both released their breath. When the elevator cleared the level, June threw a sharp elbow into Terrence's leg.

The facility's AI informed Victoria that she had arrived on the 35th floor. Unlike the other levels, which opened to an array of offices and corner lounges, there was only one set of double doors on this level. A sensor scanned Victoria as she approached, granting her access. Beyond the double doors was a seamless wall that spanned the entire level. Dead center was the floor's welcoming committee: the always smiling Lisa—a slender, middle-aged woman of Australian descent.

"Appointment?" Lisa asked.

The tone of her query made it clear she knew damn well Victoria didn't have one.

"Not today," Victoria replied.

Lisa's perfectly manicured hands stopped typing.

"I'd be happy to find a time next wee…"

"Send her in," a voice from the intercom interrupted. It prompted Lisa's famous smile.

The stark wall behind Lisa revealed an illuminated seam that became the outline of a large door. The panel slid horizontally within the wall, allowing Victoria to walk through. As she entered the grand office, the ambiance was a pleasant distraction. The entire north-west end of the office was made of glass, boasting a spectacular panoramic view of the city. It was a surreal painting of cool tones accented with pops of warm color.

"Gorgeous isn't it?" a familiar voice said.

She turned, mouth open, about to speak. The man threw up his left palm, signaling silence. Her face scrunched at his absurdity. The palm stayed up as he took his sweet time finishing his drink.

The moment the glass hit the table, he was on his feet, walking toward Victoria. His grey suit was complimented with a white collared shirt and blue suede loafers. For his age, he had unusually vibrant grey hair, that he styled like the model of the week.

"The latest reports?" he asked.

Before Victoria could respond, he had his palm up again. She exhaled, firmly, and handed him the clipboard.

"And we still haven't figured out how they got their abilities? I mean, what the hell do you people do all day?" Gradin asked.

"So far all of our theories have proven to be inconsistent," replied Victoria. "But we are close."

"Don't bullshit me, Vicky," Gradin said.

Victoria adjusted her lab coat as an attempt to maintain her composure. Gradin intensely gawked at her body before suddenly grabbing her by the neck. Seconds later she was bent over his desk.

"This is how you like it, right?" he taunted.

His hand ran up her inner thigh as he pulled her hair just enough to make her head tilt back. She seductively moaned in response when his fingers brushed past her vagina.

"Answer my questions… or no more play time."

He released his grip then spun her around to face him.

Victoria smoothed her skirt before retrieving the light pen from her inner pocket. She tapped its side as if sending Morse code.

The tip lit up brighter than before, and projected a holographic image of the human anatomy in the center of the room.

"You are aware of the chakra points in the body?" she rhetorically asked.

"Yeah I've had my share of yoga gurus during my time at Harvard," he replied.

She was used to his odd sense of humor and didn't miss a beat as she proceeded with her presentation.

"Everything in this world... me, you, plants, insects, protozoa. They all have life energy running through them. It's what some call the spirit or the soul. Think of it as an ethereal power source. It's where our personalities and emotions come from."

"So all the fancy education that taught us about brain waves and signals were nonsense, got it," Gradin said.

"Congrats on paying attention in your middle school class," Victoria replied. "If you recall, the scientific community officially recognized Gio in 2021."

She gestured toward the hologram as it depicted a stream of white light emitting through the human body. A second anatomical form appeared, but this one showed green streams of light. It had about four times the amount of light running through it. She pointed at the first digital specimen.

"This represents every human on this planet. Gio streams through the body providing access to your thoughts, feelings, dreams, etcetera. In certain situations such as traumatic stress, physical force, or even sexual stimulation, Gio may expand."

The initial bust with the white light became ten percent brighter.

"Whether internal or external stimuli, this is the highest level that Gio will flow. We've determined it's due to our human limitations. In short, we can only go as high as our bodies will allow."

"Interesting. Like a speed limit governor," Gradin added.

"Sort of."

She shifted her attention to the form with green energy.

"Now this... *this* is the Gio stream of our special patients."

"Wow," Gradin replied.

"Their bodies have a more potent, advanced level of Gio running through their system. Somehow, they're able to harness that energy, giving them their abilities. How they're able to cope with the increased energy flow, we cannot determine."

"But what we do know... pushing it too far causes the Gio stream to expand, resulting in a spike of activity in the dorsal posterior insula."

"So that explains why they freak out from time to time," Gradin added. "Shit... the pain must be... wow."

"The serum we developed assists in nerve damage repair, boosting recovery time by eighty percent. Quite frankly without the serum, they would be dead or comatose within a few months."

"This doesn't explain what happened to my mother. She's only had one incident."

Victoria sighed empathically.

"May possibly be a weaker immune system due to her age but we don't have enough data to conclude. We've noticed the Gio effect is more aggressive if the host is experiencing some form of dramatic trauma, " Victoria said.

"What was your mother going through during her episode?"

"Careful, Victoria..."

"I'm asking from a purely scientific standpoint. "

"Thank you for being straight with me. But this doesn't fully explain why my father is obsessed with these kids."

"What do you mean?" replied Victoria. "Dr. Risk is committed to finding a cure. He has done everything he can for mankind, and has refocused his life's work to help your mother."

Gradin laughed.

"He's got you all fooled. The good doctor saving the world. That's all he ever wanted."

He handed the clipboard back to Victoria and stood behind the glass desk, facing the city. The desk was spotless. On it was a laptop, a leather portfolio, and a titanium pen—all sitting parallel to the edge of the table.

"Gradin, if you tell me what happened, perhaps it can provide insight to finding a cure."

"My father knows, and what good has that done?" he interrupted.

He walked towards the cabinet, retrieved a bottle of scotch and poured himself a fresh glass. "Who do you think is the cause?"

"I had no idea. Dr. Risk's official report states he found your mother in bed."

"Of course it did."

Gradin took a marathon sip of his drink. When he brought the glass down it was empty.

"When you're a young boy, you believe anything your parents tell you. To you, they're perfect. They can do no wrong. And like all children, I thought mine were perfect too. My father's brilliance founded this company, but beneath his technological triumphs, he secretly hates humanity. The day my mother became very ill, my father devoted his life to helping her, yes. But long before that he was a man infatuated with Egyptian myths and spiritual nonsense. I once discovered a secret project to develop a level of AI that would be as complex as the human conscience. What would drive a man to create such a thing?"

"What are you saying?" asked Victoria.

"My father hates this world, because it's not perfect. Why do you think his life's work is to fix everything? My mother is the only real connection he has to the rest of us."

"Once he loses her, I can't imagine what may…"

"Why are you telling me all this?" Victoria asked.

"Soon, this will be my company. Once I prove he's out of his mind, I'll be able to persuade the board to vote him out. When that happens, I'll be in position to take his place."

Victoria seemed puzzled.

"I still don't quite understand. Forgive me, but aren't you a bit… inexperienced?"

Gradin laughed.

"The board will agree. They won't have an issue with me taking my father's place, as long as Raymond serves as my advisor. "

He sat in the chair with his back facing Victoria as he looked out over the city.

"You can leave now," he gestured. As Victoria stormed out, his mind went back to the day everything changed.

9

Elizabeth

"Gradin, where are you sweetheart?"

A mother nervously searches for her son at an extravagant soiree. The upscale mansion played host to fifty-five distinguished guests, all dressed in white. But no one was having fun. No one was enjoying the expensive wine or the lavish seven-course meal that took five chefs and a staff of twelve to prepare. Instead, everyone was huddled around the television in the great room with horror in their eyes.

The image on the screen zigzagged as the reporter frantically described her account from the news chopper.

"I can't believe what I'm seeing Mark. Several buildings on the East Side have begun to topple from the quake. You can see people fleeing their vehicles... Oh my God."

"Gradin! There you are. Have you seen your father?" asked Elizabeth, a fifty-something, post surgery brunette.

Pearls complimented her neckline, while a diamond ring with its own zip code had the pleasure of residing on her finger.

"I need to find your father. Where is he?"

Gradin was also dressed in white, but his alma mater's sweater hung across his shoulders—so everyone could be reminded he went to *that* Ivy League school. This was before his playboy days. His sterling grey hair was neatly cut. A birthmark, his mother told him.

When you born, you were so precious that God tried to take you back to become an angel. He eventually let us have you, but touched you with his might to remind us how special you are.

Gradin walked down the art-lined hallway and headed upstairs toward the study.

"Dad?" he announced as he approached the door.

He turned the doorknob but it was locked. The shriek of a woman's voice came from behind the door, followed by playful laughter. He placed his ear to the door and was startled by what sounded like things being knocked over. Gradin ran back downstairs. His mom and another gentleman were walking toward him from the opposite direction.

"Did you find your father, dear?" she asked.

Gradin didn't respond. Next to his mother was Michael Einsberg, a long-time friend of the family.

"I'm sure he's somewhere outside," Michael urged.

Elizabeth noticed Gradin's stoic expression. It raised her suspicion further. She charged towards the study and tugged on the knob twice.

"Break it down," she ordered.

"You sure, Liz?" Michael asked.

"Kick it down, now."

He hesitated, but he knew he had to be on her good side, given he would be asking for a generous 'donation' later.

Michael took three steps back and launched forward, kicking the door just above the latch. It swung open, banging against the wall inside.

"Shit! Elizabeth!"

On the chaise lounge was Gradin's father, Charles Risk, wedged between the legs of a woman who was not his wife.

"Honey, it's not what it looks like!" Charles said.

He was on his feet at this point; his shirt ruffled as he pulled his pants up.

The woman, whom Gradin had known all his life... Aunt Joy, used her arm to cover her naked breasts. Her dress was scrunched between her upper thigh and waistline. Her face... a more youthful, less plasticky version of his mother's. They shared the same facial features and hair, but her eyes were hazel.

"Liz, I'm so sorry. I'm so, so sorry," she said as she pulled her dress down.

"I thought this was over!" yelled Liz. "After counseling, I thought this was behind us!"

"Liz, please, I'm so sorry," Joy sobbed.

"And you!" shouted Elizabeth as she turned her focus toward Joy. She began breathing heavily, glaring at her younger sibling.

Joy's hair became weightless, slowly rising like a hot air balloon. The gold charm around her neck followed suit, levitating just above her chest.

"Slut! You've betrayed me for the last time!" screamed Elizabeth as her breathing intensified.

Several objects next to Joy started to rise into the air, as if no gravity existed around her. Her white high-heeled pumps hovered five inches above the mahogany floor.

"Liz. Liz is this you? Liz, are you doing this?" Charles asked.

Joy was now hovering three feet above the floor.

"It hurts! My chest!" Joy begged. "Please! Ahh! Please! I can't breathe…"

Joy's heart rate began to decline as a sharp pain pierced through it. "Liz… please…" she pleaded.

"Elizabeth!" yelled Charles.

In response, Elizabeth raised her left hand toward Charles, triggering the same weightlessness and pain in him that Joy was experiencing.

"Honey! Liz. Please," yelled Charles as he grabbed his chest.

Joy's body was now lifeless, still suspended in the air.

"Liz. Honey. Ack. Please."

Charles began to lose his breath as he swung his legs, desperate for footing, grasping his chest.

"Mom!" yelled Gradin.

Joy and Charles fell to the floor. Charles was heaving from loss of breath, but Joy lay motionless. Michael ran to her side and placed two fingers on her neck. At that point Elizabeth fainted. When she hit the floor, her arms and legs started swinging violently as if she was possessed.

She screamed out in pain as her son tried to console her. Charles looked over at Michael, who was still at Joy's side. He slowly shook his head back and forth indicating that Joy was dead.

10

CURE: Part 3

"I can't do it!" Miko yelled.

"Keep going," Robyn demanded.

They were in the rec room at one of the TRI terminals at CURE. Unlike the clean and modern aesthetic of the rest of the facility, this room resembled an old industrial loft. Polished concrete floors grounded the space while a maze of painted, exposed pipes ran along the ceiling. There were other patients interacting with the holographic terminals as well. Some were placed in a group, collectively channeling Gio through virtual objects. Each station had an experienced guide watching over the session to ensure the patients would not push themselves too far.

Robyn, one of the guides, was supervising Miko at her

station. In front of them was a levitating digital sphere with streams of Gio bouncing around within.

"I can't hold it," Miko said.

Her hands were extended towards the sphere as she tried to maintain control.

"Keep going," Robyn urged.

Even though she wasn't touching her, Miko felt a pinch over her shoulder as Robyn applied telekinetic pressure.

Across the large room, Novelle started her routine. She began to waltz across the floor like a ballerina, making her way through the other patients. She levitated above the group, held the position for a few seconds, and landed softly on her toes.

Near the entrance, June watched from his wheelchair. He couldn't make out Novelle's moves; there were others blocking his line of sight. But when she levitated above them, their eyes found each other.

"Ahhh!" Miko shrieked, breaking everyone's concentration.

"I didn't tell you to stop," Robyn reprimanded.

"I think she's had enough," Novelle said.

"She's done, when I say she's done," Robyn replied.

She thrust her hands forward, pushing Novelle back with telekinesis. Novelle caught her balance, and crouched into a defensive stance.

"Oh, you think you can take me beauty queen?" Robyn playfully asked.

June wheeled his chair over to Novelle. Before she could respond to Robyn, he grabbed her arm attempting to diffuse the situation. A jolt ran through his body, triggering a sporadic burst of images in his mind. It went too fast for him to comprehend but it heightened his emotions.

Every patient in the rec was now surrounding Robyn and

Novelle. They paced within the circle focused on each other.

"I've known girls like you my whole life," Robyn said.

"Oh yeah?" Novelle responded.

"You think you're God's gift to the world. You think you're special."

"We're all in this together Robyn. Don't do this."

"Ha," Robyn giggled.

"Me? Like you? No beauty queen. I am nothing like you or any of these undeserving brats."

Robyn stopped. Novelle was now at the opposite end of the circle—but directly in front of her.

"You may have the ability. But I am much stronger."

Robyn lowered her clenched fist to the side of her body. Her hands burst open, unleashing a force that pushed everyone back several inches. The back wall of the rec flickered, revealing the industrial aesthetic was a hologram.

Without warning, Robyn served up a triple volley of telekinetic energy toward Novelle, who was able to dodge two of the attacks and parry the third.

The circle had now split into two groups. Miko and June were in a group of six behind Novelle, while the others stood behind Robyn. Novelle raised her hands, directing her power at Robyn. Robyn felt pressure around her neck. It lasted for a few seconds before she absorbed the attack.

Robyn jerked her head forward, sending a powerful wave of energy that threw Novelle to the ground. Novelle collected herself and angrily rose to her feet. As Robyn began building up power for another attack, June restrained her.

"This ends now," June said, as a surge of anger started to build up within him.

"Easy there tough-guy," Terrence announced while grabbing June's shoulder.

June responded with a telekinetic blow that sent Terrance flying across the room.

Everyone braced for Terrence's response. But he just stood there, giving June an intense scare.

"Come on!" June yelled. "I've been waiting for this."

Out of nowhere, a piercing sound caught everyone off-guard. It was Victoria's whistle.

"Enough!" she commanded.

"You know the rules. You cannot use your abilities toward another patient."

She scanned the room, and saw that June and Novelle were in an attack stance.

"An example has to be made. The two of you," she said to June and Novelle.

"One night in solitary."

"But it was all my fault," Miko said.

"Fine, the three of you."

Three men dressed in black military-style uniforms quickly entered the hall. Each had a black stick that looked like a baton but had two quarter-inch metal prongs sticking out of the end. They escorted the three solitary-bound patients into an auxiliary elevator that took them down to the basement level. The doors opened to a tiny corridor with a large metal door. Victoria retrieved her cell from her pocket and made a call.

"Prepare solitary for three patients."

The voice on the other end said something that displeased her.

"Then put them all in one! I don't care, just make it happen!"

Victoria entered a sequence of numbers on the keypad next to the door. The door nudged and swung open. All but Victoria stepped through. As it shut, the thunderous bang startled Miko. She sniffed and clutched Novelle's wrist as the guards led them down a dark walkway.

"It's ok Miko. I'm right here."

Miko looked up at Novelle with her big, bright green eyes and found assurance in her voice.

The hall was barely lit. LEDs illuminated the path as they marched forward, revealing the scale of the space. There was no sense of a wall to the right or left, and the air smelled like it hadn't been disturbed for years. The lights only created about fifteen feet of visible space in each direction. Beyond that was an unnatural haze that clouded their perception, and piqued Novelle's interest.

"Move it," said one of the guards behind them.

At the end of the space was another door with a matte finish. It also required credentials to get through. The guard pushing June's chair punched a sequence of characters into the digital keypad, activating the retina scanner. After processing, the door slid open. On the other end was a gentleman with a more pleasant demeanor than their captors.

"I'll take it from here," he announced.

"You two," he said, pointing to the guards who weren't pushing June.

"You are excused."

He led the patients through another large room, nearly the same size as the first. This one, however, was much better lit. They could see the titanium doors to each cell had one-foot square windows. Miko walked on her toes to try to get a glimpse inside, but she was too short. The shrieks they heard from behind the doors made her jumpy.

"Ok, right here."

The cell was about twelve feet wide. It was made of the same anthracite material as June's living quarters but didn't have its pleasant lighting and color. There was only one bed in the back of the room.

"Get in."

Novelle entered first, followed by Miko. June was wheeled in afterwards. The guard came to the front of June's chair and placed his hands under June's armpits.

"Wait, wait, what are you doing?" June asked.

The guard lifted him out of the chair and placed him against the wall.

"It's cold," Miko said. "And I'm hungry."

"Try and get some rest," Novelle said.

She walked Miko over to the bed and pulled back the blanket.

June was unsuccessfully trying to find a comfortable position to sit against the wall. His stomach growled loudly enough for Novelle to hear.

"Didn't get a chance to eat, huh?"

"Huh?" he responded with a self-conscious laugh. "Oh, I'm good. Just trying to find a comfy position."

Miko found a few loose pebbles to entertain herself with, juggling them in the air without touching them. She split one of the pebbles into several smaller ones and made a smiley face.

"Can they do this? Lock us in here like criminals?" June said.

Novelle didn't respond.

Miko made one of the little rocks float toward June's ear. He didn't realize what it was and tried to swat it away like an annoying fly. It entertained Miko as she laid under the blanket watching him swat and miss.

"Stop it, Miko!" he snapped.

"Sorry," she said cringing. All the little rocks fell to the ground.

"That temper," Novelle said.

"Me?" June responded. She's the one that's out of control. And now we're stuck in here because of her," he said.

Miko stuck out her bottom lip and pulled the blanket over her head, pretending to fall asleep. A fake, pig-like snore came from under the covers.

Novelle stood up to peep through the window in the door. She couldn't make out anything except the subtle sounds of someone talking to himself. She looked back at June who was rubbing his legs.

"So what happened earlier today? Were you faking it?" she asked. June was still focused on the loss of feeling in this lower body.

"You wouldn't believe me if I told you," he replied.

"Believe what?"

"I'm still not sure it happened or if I imagined the whole thing."

"Well, we've got time," Novelle said.

"It was weird. I mean, it didn't feel weird, at least not at first. I was in my room thinking about the first time my dad took me to the city. We stopped at a newsstand to get a soda."

"But when I reached into the cooler, it was like I was there. Not my young self. Not in the memory, but me, as I am now. I somehow left my room and ended up on the street. I could smell the breeze, hear the traffic, and feel the concrete. Like I was there."

"Hm," Novelle said. She started tapping her lips with her index finger.

"Wait, are you trying to tell me that you *teleported* out of your room?"

"I don't know if I would call it that. I, I don't know. It was probably just a daydream. You know what, just forget it. I know it sounds crazy."

"Uh, hello? Look where we are," Novelle said.

"We live on the secret floor of a facility with a bunch of other people who can make things move with their minds. I think we're past the point of crazy."

"True," June nodded.

"Have you tried to do it again since? I saw a movie where this guy could like… teleport anywhere he had been once before. Sometimes he would look at a picture or something to jog his memory. Maybe thinking about your dad was the trigger."

Novelle pushed herself up and knelt in front of him.

"I thought about it, but I didn't want to go into another Gio Tantrum. I don't know if you remember how painful it is. But when I did, my entire body felt like it abandoned me. And if it happens here, it may take them too long to get the serum… if they even come at all. The thought of that alone is already making my body ache."

Novelle sat back on her butt, sliding her arms behind her.

June looked up at the ceiling.

"And I can't die in here. I can't leave my mother. I just can't. It's bad enough I've been here a year already and I haven't seen her in…"

He caught himself mid speech.

"I'm sorry. I know it's hard not knowing what happened to your family," he said.

Novelle didn't respond.

He leaned against the wall, using the ridges between the slabs of concrete to pull himself up, but his hands lost their grip, and he slid back down. He angrily slapped the floor in frustration, hurting his hand but tried to act cool.

"I still don't know how Dr. Risk found us or how he found out about me. As much as I like having these powers, I hate that it keeps me in here, away from her."

"I'm sorry," Novelle said, placing her hand on his shoulder.

"For what?" June asked.

"I know I was a bitch when we first met. Just wanted to say I'm sorry for all of that."

June looked up and smiled. "Like I could ever be upset with you," he said.

Novelle's face got red. There was a brief, awkward silence while June found the courage to ask her something that had been on his mind for a long time.

"I know this is going to sound like it's out of nowhere, but did you ever take the A train through Brooklyn?" he asked.

"Brooklyn? As in New York?"

"Uh, what other Brooklyn do you know?"

Novelle squinted and titled her head toward the ceiling. She slowly rose to her feet and walked to the opposite end of the room.

"Did I say something wrong?" June asked.

Novelle let out a deep breath. She turned around with a serious expression. Her hands were clasped together, and she nervously twirled her thumbs.

"Come on, Novelle. You're freaking me out," June said.

Novelle's fingers stopped. She sat directly in front of him, less than a foot away from his face. She placed her index finger to her lips and turned her head to listen for any sign someone may be on the other side of the door. She then leaned in closer to him.

"Have you been having any strange dreams lately?" she asked.

"What do you mean?"

"I keep having these visions where I'm in these different places. One of them was a train station but I didn't realize until now that it may have been Brooklyn. It's so hazy. Whenever I experience it, only a few things stick. The last one I had, the letter A stood out to me. There's also this woman that looks like me, but different. I think it's me, maybe in another life. But not really sure."

"Really? Like you?"

"Yeah, but like, an older me."

"Strange."

"It's like I was having an out-of-body experience. I could see myself. And I think… I don't know," she said looking away.

"What? Aww come on, don't leave me hanging like that."

Novelle paused to collect her thoughts.

"The visions have been coming more frequently, and I feel what's going to happen before it does. Not saying I'm psychic, but I feel like there's a voice guiding me. At times I can feel everything around me. I can sense when someone's in pain. But the crazy thing is… I feel like I can help them."

"Really?" June asked.

"I think telekinesis is just the beginning. I can somehow sense that we are capable of so much more. Maybe they know that and that's why we are here."

"And you still can't remember what your life was like before here?" June asked.

"It's like there's something blocking me. I have visions of what I think was my life, but I don't know if they're actual memories or just something I want to believe," Novelle replied.

At that moment, Miko, who really had fallen asleep, seemed to be having a nightmare.

"I didn't tell teacher!" she screamed in Japanese. "I didn't tell teacher!"

11

Miko

"We know you're in there Miko."

Three girls stood outside a bathroom stall in a military based Taiwanese school.

The prettiest, but deadliest of the three, Anzu, banged on each door as she made her way down the row. The other two were the Chang twins.

"Don't make me come in there Miko."

The door at the end creaked open, and out sauntered a terrified Miko. Her uniform was a little big for her. The twins giggled playfully, mocking her clothes as she crept out.

"Why are you hiding from us Miko? I thought we were friends?" Anzu said.

Her henchmen snickered.

"She's so weird."

"Yeah, super weird," they said in unison.

"You don't have to be afraid of us Miko. Here, you can have your bag back."

Anzu dangled a light brown teddy bear backpack in front of her.

"See, I told you. You have nothing to be afraid of."

Miko slowly stepped toward the girls. With each step, the girls behind Anzu let out a restrained laugh. When Miko got close, Anzu swung the bag behind her back.

"First, tell us who told teacher we were smoking in school," she demanded.

"But, I didn't," cried Miko.

"Shhhh," Anzu replied. "Don't lie to us. We. Know. Everything."

Streams began falling from Miko's eyes.

"I didn't tell Anzu, I swear."

"Aww, is it because you don't have a real family?" taunted Anzu.

"Awww…" the clones repeated, followed by more snickering.

Anzu lunged forward, seizing Miko by the neck.

"Tell me the truth! Who told teacher? Tell me now, Miko. Tell me now or I'll break your neck!"

"Crack, crack," said both of the other girls.

Anzu gave a signal that prompted one of them to exit the bathroom and keep watch. The other one blocked the entrance, just in case Miko tried to run for it again.

"No one's coming to help you, Miko. Tell me why you did it!" said Anzu as she squeezed Miko's neck tighter and tighter.

Miko pulled at her grip to no avail and kicked Anzu in the shin. It made Anzu release her.

"Bitch! I'll kill you!" Anzu announced as she grabbed the back of Miko's head and slammed it into a stall door.

Miko tried to stay down, but Anzu pulled her up and slapped her across the face. Then she dragged Miko into a stall and shoved her head into the toilet.

"Tell me! Tell me!"

Miko fought as hard as she could against Anzu's stronger physique. She dug her fingernails into Anzu's wrist until she let go.

"You little bitch!" yelled Anzu.

Miko ran past her, but the entrance was blocked. When she turned around, Anzu delivered a sucker punch to her stomach.

"Give it to me!" yelled Anzu as she reached toward the other girl.

The girl smirked, then reached into her bag and pulled out a metal rod. She handed the rod to Anzu, who never took her eyes off Miko.

Miko descended towards the other end of the bathroom. She held her stomach in pain as tears cascaded down her face.

Outside the bathroom, two spritely female students approached but quickly pivoted when they recognized the girl guarding the door was part of Anzu's gang.

"This will teach you to get in our business!" yelled Anzu. She grasped the metal rod with both hands as she charged toward Miko.

Miko closed her eyes as tightly as she could, bracing for the attack. She placed her hands over her head and tucked it between her legs. All Miko could see was the darkness behind her eyelids. There was a slight rumble, followed by eerie silence.

No giggling, no talking. Nothing. After a few moments, a sharp pain ran through Miko's body; she began to hyperventilate and her body broke into a sporadic seizure. It lasted only a few seconds before her breathing returned to normal. The whole time, fear kept her eyes closed as she pleaded to Anzu.

"Please, don't. I'm sorry. I didn't mean to tell," she whispered. "I didn't mean to."

She unexpectedly felt something on her shoulder and jerked away. But it wasn't the blow of Anzu's rod. An overwhelming draft blew over her. Slowly she opened her eyes to discover that everything around her had been destroyed.

12

Luna

"Luna. Luna?"

Luna Chenoa awoke to a streak of sunlight across her face. Her eyelids were heavy as she turned over in her comfy bed.

"Fifteen more minutes," she murmured.

The large room was littered with spare metal parts, circuit boards, monitors, and assorted tools. Along the walls hung black and white photography prints and various accolades from science competitions. Above her headboard, a framed snapshot of someone she admired, someone she had been so excited to meet last year on her seventh grade field trip… Dr. Charles Risk.

"Luna, breakfast'll be ready in ten. Luna? Luna, answer to let me know you're up."

Barbara delivered two swift knocks against the bedroom door.

"Luna, it's almost nine thirty. I gotta pick your sister up from LAX at noon, and traffic's going to be crazy."

Barbara placed her ear at the door and listened for a response, but none came.

"Luna, I'm coming in."

She jiggled the handle and swung the door open, triggering a sequence of lights that illuminated the room. She minced through the mess, making her way through Luna's robotics and science experiments.

"Luna... you can't expect me to wake you up every day."

Barbara pulled back the covers to surprisingly find a row of pillows where Luna should have been.

"Gotcha!" Luna laughed.

She leaned out of her private bathroom, toothbrush in hand. Her cackle caused toothpaste to spew from her mouth.

"Eww, disgusting."

"Aww mom, you gotta admit I gotcha this time," Luna chuckled.

She was a spitting image of her older sister, Novelle. They shared the same complexion and hairstyle, though Luna's hair was shorter and a bit more unpredictable. Her friends dubbed her Luna Einstein because of it.

"Very funny lady. Didn't you hear me calling? I probably woke up half the neighborhood," Barbara said, as she drew the curtains open.

"Yeah mom, been up the whole time."

Barbara wasn't convinced.

"Your sister's coming home today and I'm already running late. So if you still want to go, move it funny pants."

"But why is she flying into LA?" Luna asked. "Wouldn't it make sense to fly here?"

Barbara's face widened with a smile. A sigh of relief came after.

"We were gonna surprise you, but figured you would have guessed it by now."

"What mom, what?"

"Your sister will be finishing the rest of her education much closer... at USC."

"Really?" Luna said. "For real? This is the best news ever!"

She awkwardly hugged her mom and began kissing her on both checks back and forth.

"I love you two," Barbara said. "And clean up this room. It's starting to look like a boy lives in here," she smirked.

Luna rolled her eyes and ducked back into the bathroom.

"Saw that," Barbara said.

"Ugh... you see everything."

"That's because I'm your mother," Barbara responded.

Through the small window of her bathroom, Luna noticed something peculiar. She inched closer to inspect.

No way, she thought. No freakin' way!

She finished brushing, placing her mouth under the faucet head to catch the water and gargle. She dashed to her computer with the triple monitor display, and quickly logged in. On the upper right-hand corner was a weather widget. She clicked it, expanding it full screen. It stated the current temperature was 75 and sunny. She advanced to a time later in the day. The forecast was still 75 and sunny.

What the hell? This can't be right, she thought.

Three pings from her cell phone caught her off-guard. She rummaged through her messy bed to locate the phone. It dinged again, revealing its location under her pillow.

Alina: Up yet, Einstein? You're not gonna believe what I'm seeing! Hit me ASAP.

Mark: It's gnarly outside. Surprised you're not on top of this.

Chad: Holy shit dude! Are you seeing this?

Luna sprung downstairs, still in her PJs, to investigate further.

"Mom, are you seeing?"

Barbara stood frozen as she looked out toward the blue sky. Against it were concentrated specks of white. Luna approached her from behind and gently placed her arm around her. Barbara pulled her in as she reached.

"Is it… snowing?" Luna asked.

Barbara chuckled.

"You know it's been a long time since you've asked me something you didn't already know the answer to," Barbara responded. "When we brought you and your sister home, we knew we had the most amazing girls. Right away it was clear Novelle was a quiet fighter. And your intelligence quickly stood out," Barbara laughed to herself. "You were only two. Your father was reading a magazine, and you started making these noises. We couldn't make out what you were saying at first. But then, we realized you were reading the cover. You should have seen the look on your father's face when your third grade teacher recommended you skip to the sixth. I'd never seen him so proud."

Outside, snow started to accumulate. The sight was unusual, even for this time of the year in southern California. Given that none of the weather reports had predicted its arrival, the snow was a very strange surprise. They lived in a quiet suburb of Ontario, California, just off the 60 Freeway. Gradually, everyone in the neighborhood emerged from their homes, heads tilted toward the sky, perplexed by the snowfall.

"This is amazing!" Luna said.

She and her mom stepped out front to join the rest of the community. Inside, Barbara's cell phone rang several times from an unknown number and went to voicemail. A moment later, the same number called again. Luna heard the tone and headed back in to answer the call. By the time she reached the phone, the call had already gone to voicemail.

She pivoted against the marble counter to head back outside, but her phone upstairs started to ring. It was hard to miss, as it triggered both her computer and tablet as well. She bolted upstairs to take the call. It was the same number that had just called Barbara's phone.

"Hello?"

"Luna, it's me," said a distorted voice. "I need to talk to mom."

"Novelle? Novey! Hey, I just found out! USC, way to go! I'm glad you finally came to your senses. But what's with the weird number? Did you lose your phone again?"

"Luna, where's Mom? Put her on," Novelle asked.

"Novey, can you believe it? It's snowing outside. Crazy right? I mean, snow around here? In the desert? Uh… weird city. She's gonna be mad you lost your phone again though. Did it get stolen on the train? I heard they steal people's phones there. You gotta be careful Novey, especially on those trains," Luna rambled.

"Luna… mom, now!" Novelle demanded.

"She's outside, hold your horses, jeez."

Luna scrambled back downstairs. As she approached the front door, she heard the sharp, repeated tapping of vibrating glass. It was followed by a tremor that shook the entire house. Barbara was on her way back in and stumbled in the doorway.

"Luna, you ok?"

"Mom, it's Novelle."

Barbara frantically grabbed the cell phone.

"Novelle. Did you arrive? Where are you?"

There was only muffled static on the other end.

"There's an earthquake! Stay at the airport, I'll pick you up as soon as I can," Barbara said.

More muffled static.

The impact of the quake intensified, causing Barbara to lose her balance.

"Mom!" Luna yelled.

She helped Barbara keep her footing as the house continued to rumble.

Outside, the wind began to build momentum, causing the fifty-foot-tall palm trees along the street to sway back and forth. Two of the trees started to sway toward the house.

"Mom, look out!"

Luna grabbed the keys to the car and stuffed her feet into a pair of sneakers at the front door.

"I have to call your father," Barbara responded. She flicked through her phone's history and tapped a number. The phone rang and rang, but no one answered. Frustrated, she held her phone toward the ceiling.

"I'm not getting a signal," Barbara said. "Something must be going on."

They headed to the driveway and tried to enter the vehicle, but the key fob didn't work.

"The key's not working!" yelled Luna.

A loud creaking sound caught their attention. The trees began to topple.

"Mom, let's go!"

They ran into the middle of the street as two palm trees descended upon their house. One crashed onto the driveway, smashing the car in half. The other slammed through the house causing the roof to cave in. The impact evoked the front windows to shatter. The gas line behind the stove snapped, spewing gas into the home. Friction from tumbling debris triggered a spark, causing flames to ignite.

Overwhelmed by the moment, Barbara fell to her knees as other palm trees along the street began to topple towards their respective homes.

Every house on the street suffered significant damage as the colossal trunks slammed into each structure. The rumbling ground began to split apart as people fled on foot and in their automobiles. The force of the earthquake grew stronger turning the entire road to jagged asphalt.

"Barbara! Luna!" yelled a man from a black Jeep. It was Frank Brea, a big guy who lived in the neighborhood. "Get in!" he ordered, waving his hands towards the truck.

A helicopter zoomed ahead, but it was having difficulty navigating through the weather. It swerved sporadically before leveling off.

"What the hell is going on?" Luna asked.

NEIC
Golden, Colorado

William Alexander ran down the hall towards the conference room. He burst through the glass doors, interrupting Dr. Corwin mid-speech.

"Sir, you have to see this," he blurted, exhausted from the run.

Just then, Dr. Corwin's phone rang from a number he recognized. He answered.

"Dr. Corwin. Yes, this is him. May I ask who's speak…? Yes sir. Right away."

Dr. Corwin exited the room, whizzing past William. William struggled to keep up with the Doctor's rapid pace.

"I thought it was a mistake. But I double-checked. And checked again," William said. "I don't know how, but it doesn't look good."

They entered a high-tech control room filled with people analyzing data. On the left wall hung twelve monitors that collectively displayed a large graphical map of the United States. Another series of adjacent monitors displayed the entire globe. On the global map, a series of red pulsating dots highlighted points of activity. Upon entering, Dr. Corwin was greeted by John Lee, the director of the facility.

"We're tracking a spike of seismic activity along the western coast," John said.

"What else is new?" Dr. Corwin joked.

"The initial reading didn't seem unusual at first, but look at this," John said. He prompted one of the operators to display the hourly forecast on his screen. On the monitor was an infrared live feed of weather activity over California.

"Is that what I think it is?" Dr. Corwin asked.

"Yes, it is. We're online with NWS, and they've confirmed," John replied.

"The storm seems to stretch almost the entire length of the coast."

"A snowstorm? In Los Angeles? During an earthquake?" said Dr. Corwin. "I guess I've seen it all."

William cleared his throat but was ignored.

"There's more," William added, pushing his glasses onto the bridge of his nose. "I've been in contact with other agencies, and they're reporting strange activity as well. So I compared the readings from California with some of the other tremors around the globe. It didn't make sense as the signal did not originate along a fault line."

"So I did some digging and compared the point of origin for each incident."

He swiped his tablet as he spoke, then angled it toward John and Dr. Corwin.

"It may feel like it, but these are not earthquakes," William said. "See, whenever there's a quake… let's say anything from a three to a four point two, there's clear evidence of movement along the plate, which allows us to detect the point of origin. Even though the characteristics of a natural quake are similar, this activity did not begin on a tectonic level."

John was confused, yet impressed by William's findings.

"So why do you think this is happening?" he asked.

"I'm glad you asked," William smiled. He got serious again when his eyes met with Dr. Corwin's stern expression. "I was able to hack into a satellite feed at NASA and…"

"You did what?" Dr. Corwin remarked.

"I know, I'm sorry," William replied. "But I think I know where the origin is."

John and Dr. Corwin held their breath for what was going to be another one of William's high-concept theorems.

"I think these activities are a result of a significant shift in the earth's rotation."

Both gentlemen were unmoved by William's hypothesis.

"You do realize the probability of that is… I don't know… zero in one billion?" Dr. Corwin replied.

"If that actually happened William, we wouldn't be having the pleasure of this conversation," John laughed. "Everything on the earth's surface would be swept up at over a thousand miles per hour. Theoretically, the atmosphere would still be in motion with the earth's eleven hundred mile per hour rotational speed. The only survivors would be bacteria."

"But the data shows…" William pleaded. "If I could just get direct contact to NASA, I can prove it."

60 Freeway
Chino, California.

Barbara, Luna and Frank headed west on the freeway towards Los Angeles. They were cruising at fifty miles an hour until the jeep abruptly swerved, barely missing a vehicle stalled in the middle of the road. The snow had covered the stagnant vehicle completely, making it difficult to see. Luckily, Frank was able to maneuver around the car just in time.

"What's going on?" Barbara asked as they proceeded. Strangely, there were only a few vehicles on the road.

"If I can just get online," Luna added. "But my phone…"

"This any help?" Frank responded.

He retrieved a cell phone from the center console and threw it into the back seat. Luna reluctantly reached for it, making eye contact with her mom to see if it was okay.

"Ok, someone has to know something," Luna said as the phone's blue light lit up her face.

"Checking NewsFeed…"

"Shit!"

Barbara moved in her seat.

"Sorry Mom."

Barbara had strict rules about the use of language.

"Did you find anything?" she asked.

Luna didn't respond.

"Luna? Luna."

"Oh, sorry," Luna replied. "I found a video."

She positioned the phone so both Frank and her mom could see. Her finger hovered over the middle of the screen as they waited in anticipation. Luna exhaled through her nose as she tapped the play button.

"And now, our breaking news. Untimely weather has created power outages across SoCal. From earthquakes to snowstorms and tidal waves, we're experiencing what many believe to be the impact of global warming. Steven Cho, our meteorologist, has the latest."

"Thank you, Susan. If you're anywhere in Southern California, you'll be experiencing something that hasn't happened since the 1920s, a category-five snowstorm. Right now, we're projecting ten to fifteen inches of snow across LA County, the Inland Empire, even Moreno Valley. There's also dramatic seismic activity occurring in the 7.2 to 7.9 range, causing trees and some buildings to collapse. There has been no confirmed loss of life as of yet. Authorities are asking people to stay indoors and ride it out."

"Thank you, Steven. A tidal wave several stories high struck the shores of Manhattan Beach less than fifteen minutes ago. Rescue officials are en route to treat the injured. We urge everyone to stay off the beach and those residing in any coastal city to head as far inland as possible."

"But that's not all of it," Luna interrupted. "It's happening everywhere. There's a hurricane in New Jersey. A tsunami in Japan. Haiti even has a... Oh my God..."

Luna shook her head as she continued to read.

"They're reporting there was an emergency water landing of a 747 near Manhattan Beach. Oh no, the page isn't loading. We need to head back."

Frank stopped the car and tried making a U-turn, but he stalled in the middle of the road. "I'm gonna have to put it into four-wheel drive. Hold on a sec."

"Maybe if I just…" Luna mumbled as she impatiently jumped out of the Jeep.

"Luna!" screamed Barbara. "What are you doing?" Against her mother's wishes, Luna climbed onto the roof, hoping to get a stronger signal.

About twelve inches of snow had now accumulated. Winds blowing over thirty miles per hour challenged everything in its course. An SUV approached the Jeep, faster than it should have been going. Luna turned just in time to hear the SUV skid several feet before slamming into the driver's side of Frank's Jeep. The Jeep flipped onto its side and spun several yards away.

Luna was thrown from the roof and landed in the median. The snow was still fresh and soft, helping to break her fall, but the tumble knocked her out.

The driver of the SUV was disoriented. He managed to push the deployed airbags out of his way and crawl from the vehicle. Warm blood streamed down his forehead as he treaded through the snow. He could make out Frank's Jeep in the distance and headed towards it.

"Everybody okay?"

He screamed as loud as he could, but the blizzard suppressed his yelp. The wind made it difficult to reach the Jeep. When he got there, he found that Frank and Barbara's injuries were fatal. The shock of seeing a corpse caused him to collapse and the elements offered no comfort.

101

As he pulled himself up he noticed a stubborn, red strand on his sleeve. He searched the area, and found Luna's saturated hair peeking through a mound of chalky snow. She was still conscious when he got to her.

"Are you ok?"

She responded with a painful moan.

13

June: Part 2

"You gotta at least smile so people know you're ok," Ahnie said.

She had her hand extended as she took a selfie with June.

"Everybody at church has been asking for you. They'll be so happy to hear you're doing well."

June wasn't as enthused about the photo.

"You ok baby?" Ahnie asked.

"I'm good," June softly replied.

She helped him get into the car and placed the bag of clothes she brought him in the trunk.

"Nice car," he said, looking around the interior.

"Just a rental for now. I actually got the car back. They said there was nothing wrong with it but I'm having them check it again."

They drove the rest of the way home without saying a word. The car pulled into the front of the building and Ahnie turned off the ignition. They both just sat there, silent. She exhaled deeply and turned to her son.

"Don't feel the need to talk about it if you don't want to. I've tried to make sense of what happened, and all I know... is that it was God. So just take it easy. They're not expecting you back in school till next week. But if you're not ready, we can get a letter from the doctor."

June nodded.

"Ok, I'm heading in. Gonna cook some food if you're hungry."

She retrieved his bag from the trunk and took it with her into the house. She looked back at him and smiled as she entered the doorway.

Flashes of the incident conquered June's thoughts as he struggled to make sense of it.

"Mom, look out!" pierced his mind as he approached the front door. He turned the handle and a feeling of security washed over him. It was starting to finally feel normal again. Ahnie was frying onions in a skillet with peppers and various seasonings. The familiar scent led him straight to the kitchen. He entered and hugged her close.

"Wow, what's this for?" she asked, returning his embrace.

"I love you, Mom," he sobbed.

"Love you too baby."

A few days later...

"All for Jesus! All for Jesus!
All my days and all my hours!
All for Jesus! All for Jesus!
All my days and all my hours!"

The choir at Trinity Baptist Church led the congregation through a hymnal worship that rivaled the passion and intensity of a sold out pop concert. Typically lasting about twenty minutes or so, today's worship extended beyond its normal time slot, causing June to feel restless. Against his wishes, he sat in the front pew next to his mother, who could have easily worshipped for another hour had the choir willed it. She placed her hand against his leg to calm down the nervous tapping he exhibited whenever he got too anxious.

The pastor, George Davis, approached the pulpit and turned to face his disciples, but kept a special eye towards the front-left row, where June was seated.

"I really feel God wants to do something special," he stated.

The crowd responded with "Mmhm's" and "Yes's". Others nodded in agreement as a few sporadic claps emerged from around the church.

"I really feel, that God is trying to show us something special. I believe, in these difficult times, he wants to open up things to us."

"Can I get a show of hands from anyone that has been sick before?"

A few people reluctantly raised their hands.

"I don't think ya'll heard me. I said, is anyone in the house of God, that is now well, that was once not well?"

Everyone threw up their hands almost in sync. Praise and claps echoed throughout.

"You see... I believe that when you are not well, that it is not random. When you are sick, it is your body trying to tell you something is wrong," the pastor exclaimed. "How many of you know what I'm talking about?"

He paused and opened his Bible to a predetermined page marked with an orange tab.

"I would like for you to turn to the book of Proverbs, chapter three, verse five."

Those with Bibles swiftly followed direction, turning their books to the requested passage. Pastor George put on his reading glasses and began reading from a highlighted point on the page.

"Trust, in the Lord with all your heart, and lean not on your own understanding," he read. "I'll tell you how I got here."

He removed his glasses, gently placing them on the open book, as he often did for emphasis.

"I know you are all aware of the events that have taken place around the world. So, why are these things happening? Has the book of revelations come to pass? See when I read the scripture 'Trust in the Lord', I get excited. What moves me about that... is God is simply saying, lean on me. We're excited about the universe and all these incredible blessings. Everyday we try to figure out how this thing works."

"And God is saying... it's ok. I got you. The world wants us to believe the 'scientific' explanation. But science can only take you so far my friends. In that hour of darkness... in that moment of desperation. When you feel like giving up, but somehow, you find the strength to push forward. Know that it was God."

"I wish I could offer an explanation, a reason for the tragedies that have occurred over the last few weeks. My condolences to the families of the thousands that have lost their lives so quickly. I pray for the Lord to bless and cover them with strength in these difficult times. As we search for answers, we must remember that God is all powerful. And that things may not fall into our understanding, but God is infinite. In these times, we must lean onto his grace."

After the service, people gathered outside the main entrance to discuss their thoughts on the day's word, show off their church attire and gossip.

Everyone was pleased to see June. Many assembled single file to shake his hand, pray, and thank God for not only the miracle that saved his and his mother's life, but June's speedy recovery.

"Mom, think I'm gonna take the train home," June said.

"You sure baby? Dolly invited us over for lunch. Her niece Tiffany is going to be there. You remember Tiffany right? You were so close when you were little."

"Just wanna clear my head. I'll be home before dark."

"Ok. Grab your sweater from the car it's getting cold."

June was in no mood to congregate with church folk, a sentiment Ahnie said he inherited from his father. It was one of many traits they shared that she was not fond of.

The stroll to the train was the first time he was alone in a while. Even though he had been out of the hospital for several days, his mother's constant nurturing didn't allow his mind to fully settle. It felt great to be back, to know that he was missed and that people were actually rooting for him. Regret washed over June for abandoning his mother and he considered turning back, but he was now several blocks away.

No use turning back now, he thought. *Would have been nice to see Tiffany though.*

The stench burned his nostrils as he descended into the subway. He darted through, trying to escape the potent onslaught of dried urine and feces when he collided with a tourist. The woman's camera flew several feet into the air. June quickly spun and lunged towards the tumbling camera, like a wide receiver reaching for the catch with only a few seconds on the clock. He could see the Nikon fall just a few inches beyond his finger tips. But then something odd happened.

Either gravity reversed or June's hands were composed of magnetic material, the trajectory of the camera shifted, landing gracefully into his hands.

He laid on the dirty subway floor with his face buried in his bicep. To his surprise, the half magnesium half plastic camera body was safely in his hands. A group of tourists started clapping and taking pictures of June as if it was all an act.

He stood up, embarrassed yet relieved.

"Sorry about that," he said.

"Thank you. Thank you so much," the lady responded.

As he walked away, he turned back to see the group mimicking his touchdown catch, like a kid would his favorite sports athlete. He chuckled at the sight before his stomach reminded him he hadn't eaten all day.

The thought of missing out on all the good food at Dolly's seemed to amplify his hunger even further, but something else picked at his mind.

Did that really happen? How did I do that, he thought?

The overpacked train arrived. He pushed through until he found a seat against the window. He intimately examined his hands, trying to put together if what just happened was real or a hallucination. His stomach rumbled again. The thought of leaving his mother began to overwhelm his conscience. He got off at the next stop and caught a cab to Dolly's.

14

June: Part 3

The ambiance from the street awoke June. Construction consumed the block, meaning the occasional jack hammer and men shouting instructions would be the morning call for the next few weeks. A jolting sensation of panic pierced his mind when the clock next to his bed read 9:20.

"Shit, I overslept!"

He felt pain in his right shoulder from the fall he took trying to save the camera the day before. It reminded him that he wasn't expected at school for another week. He took a deep breath and turned over to face the ceiling. It felt like paradise to just lay there with no expectations or responsibilities on the horizon.

His phone chimed, notifying him of an incoming text. It was charging at the other end of the room and he couldn't muster up the motivation to get out of bed.

He reached towards the phone, concentrating on the lit screen. At first he thought... *How ridiculous*, and laughed to himself, embarrassed he even attempted such a feat. But the recent chain of events, though cloudy, suggested his idea may not be so far from reality.

He raised his hand again, this time with more intent. A subtle sensation brushed his finger tips. It felt as if he was touching the phone even though it was several feet away. He sat up in his bed, now fully awake, determined to see if this *thing* he could do was all in his head. The phone jerked to his amazement.

"Holy shit."

It was still attached to the charger, so he imagined holding the phone with one hand and the head of the cable in the other. As if he was a master puppeteer, controlling his subject, he lifted the phone into mid air, disconnected it from the charger and levitated the device toward him.

His mother's knock at the door broke his concentration, causing the phone to drop just a few inches before he could grab it.

"June, you up? I gotta run some errands but I left breakfast in the oven."

"Uh... thanks mom. Yeah, I'll be out in a second."

"Take your time, I'm leaving now. Call me if you need anything. Love you."

"Thanks mom."

June collapsed back into his comfortable sheets as his mind felt free again, knowing his mother wouldn't be around for a few hours. His thoughts jumped to the beautiful girl he noticed on the train just before the incident. He wondered if she was still taking the train and if she was still just as beautiful. He fantasized about finally meeting her and what he would say.

The lighting in the train station seemed to compliment the emotions that ran through him as she approached.

"I've been noticing you on the train," the girl seductively whispered. "I know this may seem forward, but I wanted to tell you that I'm madly in love with you."

June was dressed in a dark blue tailored suit. She, in a lovely white strapless dress. He grabbed her hand and swung her around, supporting her back as they do in the movies, and passionately kissed her. A montage of what their relationship would entail played out perfectly. His friends loved her. His mother loved her. And they lived happily ever after.

"June, you in there?"

He awoke again to his mother's knock. He didn't answer right away fearing she may be upset he hadn't left his bedroom all day, and it was now 3:46 PM.

"June? You asleep?"

His conscious advised him to stay quiet, or at least pretend as if he didn't hear her call. A moment later, the decreasing clatter of the floorboards informed that she had left his bedroom door. *Was it all a dream? Obviously the part about the girl was. But everything else too?*

He found the strength to get out of bed and dragged himself into the shower. It was exactly what he needed. After getting dressed he headed downstairs. Ahnie was in the living room reading the Bible.

"Well rested?" she asked.

Before he could answer, she jumped up from her seat.

"Let me warm something up for you to eat."

"I'm fine for now."

She insisted.

"I know you don't eat leftovers but this is still fresh. At least put something in your stomach to hold you over until I make dinner in a little bit."

"Ok," he replied.

"You slept a long time. Everything ok?" She placed the breakfast plate she made earlier in front of him. He went straight for the eggs and took two bites of the toast.

"Yeah, I must've dosed off after you left."

"That's good. Rest is the best thing for you right now."

She turned to face him and grabbed his cheeks.

"My beautiful June," she said.

June playfully rolled his eyes.

"What? You're my baby. You may be Mr. Cool Guy outside this house, but under this roof, you're my baby.

The doorbell interrupted their moment. Ahnie glanced at him.

"You gonna get that?"

He walked over to the front door, opening it without checking to see who was there.

"Surprise, negro!" said Jonas.

June turned back to see his mother throw him a wink.

"What up man?" June replied.

"Ha, you actin' like you just got out of jail or something bro," Jonas laughed. His attention quickly shifted. "Dang Miss A, what chu cooking?"

"I'll be making dinner in a bit. You boys go ahead, I'll let you know when it's ready."

They headed up to June's room.

He was happier to see Jonas than he would have thought. Something he definitely needed.

"So how you feeling man? You aight? You didn't respond to any of my texts," Jonas said.

"Tsss, man I'm good. Doctor said I was straight," June replied.

"Well that's good. Didn't wanna have to take ya girl off ya hands, you know. Coach been asking when you coming back. You know regionals only two weeks away. You gonna compete?"

"I'm still trying to gather my strength chief. But we'll see."

"So what happened man? I heard the accident was crazy."

"Damn kid, a brother just got home. Didn't know I was gonna be on Oprah and shit."

Jonas laughed.

"But for real though. For you and moms to walk away without a scratch, that's pretty dope man. Someone must have had ya'll back. You think your pops…"

June's eyebrow arched, causing Jonas to pause mid sentence.

"I mean, your pops must be… sorry man. I'm just glad to see you in one piece bro." He paused. "You know sometimes I just be saying too much."

"Don't even trip. I appreciate you fam," June assured him.

"Look man, my bad about that whole test thing. I just didn't know how to deal."

"Don't worry about it," June added. "It's nothing. Next time just study, dumbass."

Jonas cracked up.

"They must've gave you some comedian pills in the hospital or something. Out the blue, you Mr. Funny Guy now. But forget all that, look what I got," Jonas said.

He reached and grabbed something tucked into his belt behind his back.

"BOOM! Madden 2024 bruh!"

"Aww it's on. You brought your controller?"

"Come on man, you know I'm always ready."

Downstairs, Ahnie had the news in the background as she prepared dinner.

"Authorities are still sifting through the rubble. An official statement from the mayor's office said it could take up to twelve weeks to fully repair the damage."

Upstairs, June and Jonas engaged in a friendly competition of Madden football. It was as if they had no time apart.

"Look bruh, I know you just got back and everything. But there's a crazy jumpoff tonight in Brooklyn. I knew your mom would trip if I brought it up earlier, but I'm telling you man it's gonna be off the chain," Jonas said.

"Word? A party? Who's throwin' it?"

"Man, when the earthquake shook Manhattan, some of it hit Brooklyn too and…"

"Earthquake? What earthquake?" June asked.

"You kidding me right?" Jonas asked.

June's serious scowl showed he was not kidding.

"Wait. You mean to tell me you have no idea about the biggest earthquake to hit the east coast? In like, for-ever? I mean all this crazy shit happened all over man. People think it's on some global warming shit."

June still seemed puzzled.

"Wow, you're really serious."

"Yeah yeah, so what about this earthquake? And what does this have to do with the party?" June asked.

Jonas still couldn't believe June didn't know about the earthquake.

"Man, it's crazy you have no idea about this. Like five hundred people died or something. Even the Lincoln Tunnel cracked man. Whatever they gave you in there, sign me up for that shit."

"You crazy man," June said.

"Ok, so check this. An office building in Flatbush was declared unsafe, so they moved everybody out."

"Let me guess, this is where the party is gonna be. That's smart," June said.

"Man you ain't let me finish."

"Ok, ok, go ahead."

"Thank you sir. Ok so a girl I know's company used to be in that building. They've been operating out of a remote location for the last week and she tells me they just declared the building safe again. But their office is in no rush to move back. Something about there's still some official paperwork blah blah blah and insurance for everything they lost. But as far as they know, the building is safe. And it's a dope spot man, so…"

"So you're gonna throw a party there before they move back in," June said.

"Exactly. The building's empty. No one to call the cops, we charge ten dollars a head, and we make this money. And..." Jonas tapped June on his arm." We celebrate my boy coming home. It's a win-win."

June face palmed and looked at Jonas through his fingers. "You must be out your mind."

"C'mon man. Just tell moms we going to my crib to play video games or something. Say you wanna spend time with your friends to keep your mind off things. She won't say no, trust. Ha ha. See what I did there?"

June rubbed his right eye and looked up at the ceiling. Then back at Jonas. Then at the ceiling again.

"So, you want me... after just being home for a few days after I was in the hospital for a week... to take my mom's car... and go to some crazy ass party in Brooklyn... that's happening in a building that was hit by an earthquake?"

"Well when you make it sound like that... but it'll be a good way to get back into the swing of things. Everybody and they moms gonna be there," Jonas urged.

"You my boy and everything, and we've done some crazy stuff but I think you may actually be crazy on this one Jonas. I mean, I just got home... ain't even take my damn shoes off yet. Still trying to put my head together. And you hitting me with this? I just don't know man."

"Boys, food's ready!" yelled Ahnie from the kitchen.

The dining area was modest. A traditional style cherry walnut table with seating for six stood in the center, with a matching wall unit holding family photos of June, his mother, and other relatives.

"This is good, Miss A," said Jonas as he smacked his lips. "I say it again… I never thought I would like African food, but the stuff you cook make me not wanna eat anything else."

"Thank you Jonas," Ahnie replied. She hated being addressed as Miss A.

"This is more of a Southern dish. Just some fried fish with gravy, onions, and peppers."

June nodded.

"Food ok son?" Ahnie asked.

"Yeah, food's good. Always good mom," he said with a mouthful.

"This food is soooo good," Jonas said as he threw down his fork.

"Hey June, I got that new Madden for PlayStation 8 man. You should come through and check it out real quick. I mean, if that's cool with you Miss A."

June slowly threw his eyes at Jonas while shaking his head.

"Of course it's cool," said Ahnie in a *I'm just as cool as one of you kids* tone.

"Really?" June said.

"Of course, sweetheart. Go have some fun with your friends. I know you don't want to be cooped up in this house with me all night. Plus you been sleeping all day. Go ahead. Have some fun."

June sat in awe. He decided to push it a bit further. "So is it cool if I take the car?"

"I think the bus is a better idea. But call me when you're ready, and I'll come get you if it's too late."

"Still can't believe this is happening," June said. "I can't believe she didn't see right through us."

Jonas laughed. "Remember when I sprained my ankle all crazy after regionals last year?"

"Yeah?"

"Man that joint hurt, but my mom did any and everything bro. Even wild stuff she always said no to, she was all of a sudden cool with. When you hurt, all mothers care about is making you feel better. Trust me bro. If you gonna try shit, this is the time to do it. Take advantage, my brother. Take advantage."

"Sometimes you're too smart for your own damn good," June replied.

"You lucky we boys man, I'm dropping knowledge I usually charge muh-fukas $59.95 for."

June laughed.

"You crazy man."

They got off the train and walked a half mile east towards a row of industrial office buildings. None of the windows were lit up.

"You sure we in the right place?" June asked.

"Def," replied Jonas. "Matter of fact, wait here real quick."

Before June could object, Jonas was already headed into the alley between two of the buildings. The streetlight was just bright enough to light the first few feet into the alley. Beyond that, it was pitch black. June slowly crept toward it.

"Jonas, " he whispered.

"Jonas!"

"Jonas!"

The only other sound was the muffled bass from a black car down the street.

Can't believe this dude got me out here, he thought.

The bass from the car got louder then vanished, followed by the slamming of three doors.

June turned around to see three figures walking toward him. One was much larger than the other two and their faces were dark. He squinted to see if they looked familiar. The smell of cigarettes reached him before they did.

"This the place?" asked the girl as she took a drag and exhaled. The left and right side of her head was almost completely shaved. Long straight hair hung down the right side of her face. The other two were guys. One with a buzz cut and the other with a style similar to the girl, except his hair was much shorter and slicker.

"Hello?" asked the girl.

June realized he was in a daze.

"Hello?" she asked again. "Is this the place?"

The fact that Jonas wasn't back yet held his attention and he was beginning to get very annoyed.

"Hell if I know," he replied.

She smiled, took another hit of her cigarette and stepped closer to June, her voluptuous figure and strong scent of the cigarette caught him off-guard. He found his eyes locked onto her perfectly round breasts.

"Well, do you know how to get in?" she asked.

June missed the question.

"I'm sorry, um, yeah. I mean… I don't know. I think so," he replied. "My friend just went down the alley, but I'm sure once he gets..."

"Let's go Liz," shouted one of the guys. "I think you get in this way."

The two guys walked into the same alley that Jonas went into. The girl followed but stopped right before she was completely out of the light. She turned around, took a final drag and flicked the butt away.

"See you inside," she said with a playful wink.

Twenty minutes went by, and Jonas still wasn't back. June walked back and forth past the alley hoping Jonas would soon pop out. At first he was worried, but now he was upset that he again had fallen victim to one of Jonas' schemes.

You know what, screw it, he thought.

He furiously stomped into the dark alleyway. His confidence dwindled with the decreasing available light. He walked a few yards in until he could hear the faint sound of music. It was so subtle he wondered if he was actually hearing it or if it was in his head. Either way, it gave him enough confidence to press forward.

Shoulda just stayed my ass home, but nooooo.

He took a few more steps and the music went away, taking with it his remaining confidence.

What the hell, he thought. *Ok June, keep it together.*

He tried to see his hands in front of his face, but couldn't.

Ok, breathe. Focus. Definitely heard something a few steps back.

As he pivoted, a creaky metal sound came from behind him. A door opened causing red light to spill into the alley.

"Yo is that you bro?"

"Jonas?" June nervously asked.

"Nah, your baby daddy," Jonas responded. "Bring your scared ass in here man. All the hunnies asking for you."

A sense of relief washed over June. Then he remembered to be angry. As he walked past Jonas, he bumped his shoulder.

"This nig-"

A succession of red bulbs lit the way. The music grew louder when they turned the corner, which led to a freight elevator. Jonas pressed the button.

"Damn, someone must be coming down."

"Man how you gonna just leave me out there like that?" June asked.

"You buggin' man. I left you for five minutes," Jonas replied.

"Five minutes? Really dog? You gonna stand there and tell me you were gone for five god damn minutes?"

"Calm down bruh. You wildin' right now," Jonas said.

"Don't tell me to calm down!" yelled June as he got in Jonas' face. The lights in the hallway flickered. His face was now only an inch or two from Jonas'.

"I just got out the damn hospital! I should be at home right now resting and shit. But the great mastermind Jonas Florence decided that was not going to happen. I mean, do you even think about the shit you do before you do it?"

The light flickered more aggressively as though it synced with June's speech.

"I mean, do you?"

June was breathing hard with his fists clenched tight. The elevator finally arrived with a group of disorderly teens.

"This is the most awesome party ever!" shouted one of the guys. They walked back out toward the alley laughing and carrying on.

Jonas didn't say a word. He stepped into the elevator, pressed #2, and stood with his hands crossed in front of him.

"Well, you coming?"

June was still angry. His mind was telling him to walk out right then and there. But his curiosity, and the idea of seeing the girl in the alley coerced him onto the elevator. The door shut and the elevator went up. Neither said a word. As it approached the second floor, the music grew even louder than before. Jonas stepped out after it settled and raised the door, holding it for June.

"You coming?"

June stepped out under it. They walked through a set of double doors down another hallway. The music was much clearer at this point. The beat was fast paced and familiar to June. Another set of double doors confronted them. Jonas grabbed the handle then took a breath and looked back at June.

"Look, I just wanted to chill with my boy you know. But just say the word and we could head back right now."

June looked at Jonas with a 'you bullshittin' expression.

"I'm serious June. Say the word and we out. I'll even tuck you in and make sure you take your vitamins."

June chuckled. "Man, I really hate you sometimes," he said with a smile.

"There he is," Jonas said. "Mr. angry man is gone and my boy's back."

June laughed. "You had me heated man. I was like, who does that?" he said with his arms open.

Jonas rushed June with a hug and lifted him off his feet.

"We like brothers man."

"All right, all right, all right. Just put me down."

"Not till I shake that temper out of you."

"I'm cool, I'm cool."

"You sure?"

"Yeah man, I'm straight."

"Aight."

Jonas put him down and loosened his embrace. He turned to face the door and put his arm around June.

"Some baddies in here man. You bout to have the best welcome back party in the history books."

Jonas opened the door and the music rushed their ear drums. The bass shook through June's body as they walked through the crowd. The room was the size of an empty warehouse. The windows were covered and large industrial fans spun above, sending a cool breeze throughout the space. The ceilings were about twenty-five feet high with exposed piping running along them. The entire space had a purplish tint with flashes of green and blue rotating orbs. Jonas pointed toward the DJ booth as if trying to catch his attention. The DJ seemed to respond and lowered the music. He grabbed the microphone and spoke.

"Everybody, give a shot out to my man, June! He was out of commission for a minute, but we're glad to have him back!"

The spotlight found June and the crowd went wild. As he pushed through the event, everyone patted him on the shoulder. Women rubbed his chest and thrusted their butts into his thigh as he made his way through.

The scene seemed to slow down to a crawl as if he was in a music video.

"See, they all showing you love. This is for you man," Jonas said.

June was speechless. He smiled and raised a fist to give Jonas a dap. Instead Jonas stuck his hand straight out for a handshake. They shook and embraced.

"I appreciate you man," June said.

"No doubt fam. I figured sooner or later you'd come in, and we would surprise you. Then I remembered how you scared of the dark and shit," Jonas replied.

June shook his head and smiled. "Whatever."

They walked through the crowd toward a section that was roped off. There was a large man standing next to the rope. As Jonas approached, he opened the path to the lounge area. There were a few people hanging out, drinking and conversing. Jonas noticed something caught June's attention and decided to do something about it.

"Hey let me introduce you to…"

The girl that was outside earlier stood up and introduced herself.

"I'm Liz."

She held her seductive gaze on June.

"Oh you two already met?" Jonas asked.

"We go way back," replied Liz with a wink.

"Well, I'll let you two get re-acquainted. I got people to do and things to see," he said before vanishing into the sea of people.

"Don't worry, I'll take care of you. Want a drink?" she asked. As if his answer would have mattered.

"Nah, I'm straight," June replied.

She smiled and took a sip from her red cup.

"Try this."

June reluctantly reached for the cup. He looked inside while swirling it around, and paused to look back at her before taking a sip. The drink was smooth at first but burned when it hit his chest. He wasn't going to let her know that though.

"It's good," he said with a nod. "Strong, but smoov." He caught himself before asking what it was. It was beginning to make him slightly uncomfortable that Liz was not taking her eyes off him.

Which one of those guys she came with is her boyfriend? Better play it cool. And where is this cat Jonas?

He took another sip from the cup and before he could finish swallowing she had another request.

"Dance with me!" she said. Without waiting for a response, she grabbed his wrist and led him into the crowd. It was like walking through a dancing cornfield. Even though the music was blaring loud, June thought he heard a crackling sound.

"Do you hear that?" he asked.

"Yeah, this DJ's dope as shit right?" Liz said.

"No. I mean, do you hear that noise?"

"What?"

"There's a noise! Like something's breaking!" June repeated.

He scanned the room to find where the sound was coming from. "You can't tell me you don't hear that," he said pointing towards the ceiling. Everything started to appear more vivid. The light beams swirling around the warehouse seemed to be moving at light speed, yet he could still make them out. They made patterns on the ceiling that seemed to grow organically like a wall of vines.

"Come on, dance with me," Liz said.

She seemed even more beautiful than before. Her hips and the baseline were in sync as she gyrated to the music. June found his hands on her hips with her back towards him. She thrusted her butt into his lap, swaying back and forth to the rhythm of the drums.

June could feel her body's energy flow into him. He felt a warm sensation in his fingertips as they brushed against her hips. A purple glow began to emit from her. It was vibrant. It moved around her, flowing like a wave and returned to her body. The crackling sound brought him out of the haze. But he could still see her aura.

What the hell? June thought as he stepped back from Liz. The purplish aura was still with her, but now everyone in the room had it.

I've gotta be going crazy. He stumbled through the crowd heading toward the VIP area. Everyone there also had a purple glow. A sudden pain struck his forehead and he found himself feeling disoriented.

"You ok?" asked the bouncer in front of the VIP lounge.

"Where's the bathroom?" June asked.

"The men's bathroom is to the right of the DJ booth," replied the bouncer.

"Damn, that's at the opposite end of the room."

Uneasiness took over his stomach. He held it with one hand and used the other to pierce through the crowd. Halfway through, he bumped into Liz again.

"You ok? Don't tell me you're already drunk," she asked. He wanted to respond but couldn't find the strength. Beyond the DJ booth, as the bouncer had stated, was a red door. He pushed through it to discover a dark hallway.

This freakin' place. It's a damn House of Horrors.

The hallway was just bright enough to see where he was going. It was long and veered into a sharp left causing him to stumble. Finally, he saw a door with 'MEN' lit up. He was so relieved, he leaned against the wall next to the door to catch his breath and celebrate. He might have stayed there for a while if the two guys exiting hadn't almost crushed him with the door.

"Jesus Christ!" yelled June.

Both guys looked at him as they walked off like he had done something wrong. The bathroom was surprisingly clean, except for the overflow of paper towels in the trash bin. The cold water felt good on his hands. He waited till they were halfway full of water and splashed his face. And again. He looked in the mirror and noticed something different about his eyes. Leaning forward, he used his fingers to spread open his eye socket. The bass of the music caused the mirrors to slightly vibrate. He wasn't able to focus clearly. He shut his eyes, which amplified the noise. When he opened them, he didn't recognize the reflection that was staring back at him.

A loud thump, followed by a barrage of men arguing derived from the WOMEN's restroom across the hall. A swarm of clacking heels followed. The commotion snapped June back into consciousness.

"Where the hell is our money?" someone shouted, just before the door slammed shut.

June peeked into the hallway. After all the women were gone, he crept across the hall and placed his ear against the metal door.

"I'll have it tomorrow. On my word," said a voice that sounded oddly familiar.

Jonas? June thought.

"That's what you said three weeks ago! Then we hear you're throwing a party?" said another.

"You'll get your money tomorrow. I swear."

"Well we better Jonas. Cause I've lost my patience!"

June heard footsteps moving closer to the door and slid back into the MEN's room. The two guys who were with Liz earlier stormed out. June waited a moment before dashing across the hall.

There was Jonas, sitting against the far wall, hunched over. His right eye was bruised and he was holding his stomach.

"Jesus Jonas, what's going on?" June said.

"It's cool," replied Jonas. "It's cool bruh. Everything's cool."

"What was all that about?"

"Oh, that? That was nothing. Just some clowns trying to be tough guys and shit. They watch one season of the Sopranos, now they gangstas."

June helped him to his feet and walked him to the sink. He dampened some paper towels and tried to wipe the blood off Jonas's face.

"Whoa, whoa. What you doing?" Jonas asked.

June snapped his head back, confused.

"Gimme that," Jonas said. He grabbed the paper towel from June and began wiping his face. He rinsed his mouth with water and spat blood into the sink. He recovered a pair of sunglasses from his jacket's inner pocket.

"See? All good brother."

June stood there shaking his head in astonishment. Jonas limped toward the exit, patting June on the back as he passed him.

"You coming? There's a party going on out there," Jonas said.

"You're crazy man," June laughed. "Off the charts crazy."

The party was going full steam. June scanned the crowd for Liz. He didn't see her, but he noticed one of the guys from the bathroom heading toward the exit. He followed him with his eyes until he saw the other one aggressively grabbing Liz's arm.

She pulled away, spilling his drink. He reached back and slapped her across the face. Liz fell to the ground.

Who do these guys think they are?

June took a step forward but was blocked by Jonas.

"Leave it alone, man," Jonas said. "Leave it alone."

He took a long look at Jonas who was still holding his stomach in pain. He was talking, but he couldn't hear what Jonas was saying. He wasn't even hearing the music anymore. All he could feel was the fire building inside of him. His attention was solely on the two guys and Liz as they exited the party. A few seconds passed before June could hear the music and Jonas again. He took a breath, brushed Jonas' hand aside and headed through the crowd toward the exit. Jonas tried to follow, but his injury made it difficult.

The crowd seemed to part as he made his way through, arriving at the elevator only a few seconds after Liz and the two men.

"I don't think she wants to go with you," he announced.

The one with the slick hair turned around. He was much bigger than June had remembered. "And you think she wants go with you, asshole?" he asked.

"Leave him alone Dante," Liz said.

"You shut your mouth bitch," Dante ordered.

A fire sparked in June, and he found the courage to take a swing at Dante. He caught him off-guard, which was more effective than the punch itself. Still, it barely moved Dante's muscular 6'3" frame.

"That's all you got, superman?"

Dante delivered two quick jabs to June's face and an uppercut to his chin. June stumbled back, dazed.

The other guy holding Liz's arm cackled like a wild hyena. "You got him, bro."

"Not yet, but I will," replied Dante. "Gimme the heat."

"Dude," said the other guy. "He's down, forget about it."

"Give it now!"

"Shit man! I'm not trying to kill anybody tonight."

"I'm not going to ask you again, Kelly. Give me the gun."

"C'mon Dante. Why you have to say my real name?" He reached inside his jacket and handed Dante a black 22-caliber pistol.

Dante grabbed the gun and lightly slapped Kelly in the face twice, like they do in the mobster movies. Then he spun around and aimed the gun at June.

"See, I could take your life right now, you little bitch," Dante said. "You know what happened to the last guy who touched me?"

June squirmed, swaying out of the way of the gun.

Dante removed the clip and held the gun near the nozzle as he approached June. "You're about to find out. Should've minded your own business," Dante said.

He raised the gun and struck June across the face. Blood spewed from June's mouth.

He felt his body go limp, but somehow, didn't fall. Dante was holding onto his shirt, preventing him from falling to the floor. Before he could look up, Dante swung his hand back and smacked the gun across June's face again. It made a cracking sound as the metal hit June's skull. Dante let go of June's shirt, and he fell to the ground.

June's mind flashed to the day of the event, a moment before a truck would have almost killed him and his mother. Except this time, he was standing outside the car. He watched in horror as their car cruised through the intersection, without knowledge of the impending danger.

June saw the entire accident unfold before him. He could see his aura transform from purple to a greenish color. It extended from his hand, creating a force field that stopped the truck. The scene paused at that moment. June examined every detail until he reached the force field. It pulsated when he touched it, releasing energy back into his finger. It shot down his arm. A painful, burning sensation rushed through his veins, but along with it came a sense of power. A power he had never felt before.

June came to and found that his aching face was resting on the dirty floor. The slightest sound was now uncomfortable. The vibration of Dante and Kelly's voices were torture. The clank and drag of metal as the elevator approached was even worse.

Kelly was still restraining Liz as Dante found amusement over what he had just done to June.

133

"See Kelly, that's how you knock a mutha-fuhka out."

They all had their backs turned to June as the elevator settled. Dante stepped forward and lifted the freight doors. Kelly pulled Liz in and pressed the button for the ground level.

Dante looked through the exposed shaft and saw June was making his way to his feet as the elevator descended. June's angry gaze seemed to illuminate the dark corridor as his eyes met Dante's. As the elevator cleared the level, Dante stuck up his middle finger at June.

Liz was still being manhandled as the trio made their way through the dark alley. Once they cleared the building, Kelly let go of Liz's arm.

"Get your ass in the car," Kelly demanded.

Liz scowled defiantly, but did as she was told. Dante retrieved a pack of cigarettes from his jacket and pulled one out. Kelly, without instruction, lit the tip of it. The temperature had dropped a few degrees, causing Dante's breath to form a thick cloud of smoke as he exhaled.

"Colder than polar bear pussy out here," Kelly remarked. He rescued a blunt from the corner of his inner pocket and lit it up. He and Dante casually leaned against the car enjoying their smokes as if the evening's events were nothing but daily routine.

"Think you might have killed that guy?" Kelly asked.

Dante took a glacial drag from his cigarette and tilted his head back to exhale. The full moon provided most of the light on this side of the building. He made a circle with his thumb and index finger, encompassing the moon while peering though like a telescope. "Nah, I saw him get up."

"Shit, really?" Kelly responded.

"Thought he was dead for sure."

Dante took one last drag and flicked the still-lit butt into the street. Kelly did the same as he entered the driver's side of the vehicle. A jet-black Mercedes sedan with gunmetal wheels and tinted windows. The exhaust growled when he turned the key.

"Let's get outta here," Dante said. He turned and leaned into the back seat toward Liz.

"Still love me, baby?" he playfully asked.

"Screw you!" she replied.

Kelly drove a few yards ahead and made a U-turn. As he completed the turn he began to speed up, but stopped abruptly.

"What the hell, dude?" Dante asked.

Kelly didn't respond. His attention was fixated on something in front of him. He leaned forward, squinting his eyes to make out what it was. His hand slowly left the gearshift as he pointed out the windshield. "Look at that," he said.

A few yards ahead of the car stood June. His fists were clenched at his side, head tilted down and shoulders up, like a bull ready to charge.

"This guy can't take a hint," Kelly laughed. "What did you put on this one, Liz? He's crazy for ya."

Dante peered though the windshield for a moment and slowly turned toward Kelly.

"Run his punk ass over."

Kelly exhaled through his nostrils as his grip tightened against the steering column. His brows lowered as he revved the car. The engine roared like a mechanical monster primed for attack.

Kelly slowly cocked back his right foot, releasing the brake.

It hovered just above the gas pedal. He exhaled again and slammed into the throttle. The car leapt forward but moved only a few inches—its tires screeching madly as the engine revved. But it wasn't going anywhere.

"Dude, what are you doing?" Dante asked. "Take this mother-fuhka out!"

"The car. It won't move," Kelly replied.

Impatient, Dante swung his left leg over the center console and pressed his foot over Kelly's, which was already hard on the gas. The car revved louder but still didn't move.

"I'm gonna end this now," Dante said. He grabbed the gun from his waistband as he hopped out of the car. "If you wanted to die tonight, you came to the right place my friend."

June spread his fingers, freezing Dante in his tracks. Dante grabbed his own neck with both hands, dropping the gun. Kelly and Liz looked on, not sure if what they were seeing was real. As June lifted his hand towards the sky, Dante simultaneously lifted from the ground, gasping for air.

"Let the girl go," June said.

At this point, Dante was suspended three feet off the ground.

Kelly threw his head sideways, signaling Liz to exit. She sloppily crawled out and ran into the alley. June's nose started to bleed as he focused on keeping Dante suspended. Kelly noticed that the car had inched forward when Liz got out and applied more pressure on the gas.

The tires peeled as it sped toward June. A moment before the car could strike him, June pointed both of his palms toward the car, stopping it a foot away. The tires continued to spin as the rear end of the Mercedes lifted off the ground.

With his left hand still facing the vehicle, June brought his right hand back and thrust it forward. The front half of the Mercedes crumpled like an empty paper bag. This killed Kelly instantly, crushing him between the steering column and front seat. It happened so quickly, Kelly didn't even have a chance to scream.

June dropped his hands and hunched over, exhausted. Dante fell to the ground panting for air. He crawled for the gun that had tumbled a few feet away. Without hesitation, he pointed the weapon and fired. June instinctively raised his hands to protect himself. A green spark flared where the bullet would have struck him.

"What are you?" Dante asked as he stood up.

June could barely lift his head to see the gun pointed at his temple. A sensation raged throughout his body—the same he had felt that day when he did the impossible to save his mother's life.

Dante had the gun pointed squarely at June's temple, his finger poised on the trigger. He turned back to see the mangled vehicle with Kelly's corpse inside.

"You... you killed him. You killed my brother," Dante said. "Look at me. Look at me!"

Dante pushed the gun's barrel into June's forehead.

"I'm gonna find anyone you ever cared about and do to them what you did to my brother," Dante said. He kicked June onto his back and cocked the pistol.

"See you in hell, asshole."

Two gunshots echoed through the warehouse district. Dante fell on his side with the gun still in his hand. A few yards away in front of the alley stood Liz, Jonas, and one of the club bouncers.

Jonas had the warm gun in his hand as he ran to June.

"You ok, man?" Jonas asked. He reached down to help June to his feet.

"Yeah, I'm fine," June replied.

"What happened out here?" Jonas asked.

"I don't know. I guess I must have…"

They could hear sirens approaching.

"Shots fired! Shots fired! We are engaging the suspects in the warehouse district, Morningside and 120th. All available units! I repeat Morningside and 120th St."

Tires screeched to a halt as the officers pulled up, immediately drawing their weapons. Jonas, not realizing the gun was still in his hand, turned around to point at Dante, who was on the ground.

"Hey, he's the one you want!" he shouted. One of the officers fired, striking Jonas in the chest.

15

A Doctor's Visit: Part 4

"So, you're saying my son is like one of these... people?" Ahnie asked.

"Yes, Ahnie. That's why it's crucial we get him to CURE so he'll have the chance to live a full life. You see, the condition June has allow him to do special things— great things. Which is the reason you were able to survive your incident. But the side effects cause tremendous damage to the body. And without proper treatment, he may not make it to his next birthday."

"This is a lot to take in Charles. You can't expect me to just believe there is a connection because my son and your wife share the same color eyes."

"I understand, which is why I want to invite June to come down to CURE. Just to take a few tests… with your permission of course. You'll get all the information you need then."

"If what you're saying about my son is true, I don't want him to be the subject of some experiment."

"Not at all. I give you my word on that, Miss Abena. In addition to the care we provide, we'll also give June a safe environment where he can learn to control and understand his abilities, with others like him."

Ahnie still seemed unmoved.

"I give you my word that he will be taken care of," Charles assured. "Also, all of this comes at no cost to you."

Ahnie sighed, stood up, and walked to the front door. "Thank you Doctor. I'll discuss this with my son."

Charles opened his mouth to speak but caught his words before they left his throat. He stood up and grabbed his briefcase. "No problem. I'll have my assistant follow up with you. Let's say, in a few days?"

His phone rang.

"Excuse me," he said as he pressed the screen to answer. He turned his back to Ahnie to take the call. "Are you sure? … Has Terrence clarified this? … And he thinks it's one of them? … Interesting. Ok, I'm on my way." Charles tucked the phone into his jacket pocket and turned back to Ahnie.

"Where is June?" he asked.

"At his friend's house," she replied.

"Are you sure?"

"Why?"

"I'm sorry, Ahnie, but I'm afraid June may be in some trouble."

Jonas laid face-up in the middle of the street. His black t-shirt was drenched in blood. The officer who fired the shot stood a few yards away with his gun pointed toward them.

"Put your hands behind your head and lay on the ground!" he ordered.

"Don't die on me, man," June cried as tears welled up in his eyes.

Jonas coughed up blood as he tried to speak, "Can't believe that pig shot me bruh."

"You gonna be aight man. You gon' make it."

June turned toward Liz and the bouncer. "Call 911!" he screamed.

Jonas coughed again, revealing a bloody smile. "You always had my back. Even when I didn't have yours."

"Don't even trip. We're brothers," June said.

Another patrol car arrived. An officer whose badge read *McNamara* stepped out of the vehicle. He addressed the other two officers immediately.

"What the hell happened here?"

"They robbed a liquor store on one-fifteenth. We got the call. Two guys and a girl wearing all black. While searching the area we heard gunshots from this direction. We arrived and one of them was armed. He turned toward me, and I fired," said the officer with a heavy breath.

"Shit!" McNamara said. "I know these kids. They're on the track team with my son. Is the weapon still on 'em?" he asked.

"Has to be."

"Ok but don't fire your weapon," Officer McNamara said.

Jonas' eyes started to slide shut. "I ain't even get to meet your girl man. Was gonna look fly at ya'll wedding too."

June held Jonas tight as he fought to hold back his tears. "Don't die on me man," June said. "You can't… I can't lose anybody else."

Jonas' eyes were still open, but he was no longer responding.

"Jonas. Jonas, talk to me," June said as he shook his friend's lifeless body. "Jonas…Jonas!"

"June, this is Officer McNamara!" the cop yelled over the loud speaker. "I need you to put your hands behind your head and lay face-down on the ground."

June's vision was blurry from tears as he lifted his head. He was now completely surrounded by flashing red, white, and blue lights. He gently set Jonas' head on the concrete.

He recalled a scene from a movie where a man closed the eyes of his dead comrade as a sign of respect. He did the same for Jonas.

"June, this is Officer McNamara! I need you to put your hands on your head and lay face-down on the ground!"

June slowly placed his palm on the concrete to push himself up. There were a total of eight police officers on the scene now, five of them with their guns drawn.

"Get down on the ground!"

"Get down now!" they all screamed.

June wiped the tears from his eyes and looked down at Jonas. A memory of his dad flashed in his mind.

June was only eight the last time his dad was deployed. The car was loaded, just like the other times. June watched his dad kiss his mother and whisper that he loved her.

He walked over to June, placing his hands under his armpits. "Ok, let's see if I can lift you up," he said. He pretended to struggle as he tried to lift June off the ground.

"You're getting heavy son."

June laughed. It was something his dad did every time he left for a long trip.

A single tear rolled down June's face. He tried to turn away, but his dad whisked him up. "What you crying for? You're the man of the house now. Can't be crying," he said as he tickled June. June giggled, wiping away the tear.

"Dad, why do you have to go?"

His father smiled. "Listen June," he said. He placed June down on the ground and crouched so they were at eye level.

"You see, God chose some of us to look out for everybody else. We are the ones who have to make sure that people who can't protect themselves are safe. It is a responsibility we are called to."

He smiled and kissed June on the forehead. June felt as if he was being touched by the sun.

"You are strong, my child. And one day you'll be much stronger than me. But that strength, that power inside you..." he said as he touched June's chest. "It's not for you. That power is for others. For those who cannot fight for themselves."

The sound of officer McNamara's voice brought June back to the scene.

"Put your hands behind your head!" he commanded. "Now!"

June slowly spread his arms open. His father's words were all he could hear.

As if he was trying to squash a fly right in front of him, he slammed his hands together. It created an invisible force that pushed all the officers back several feet. Their patrol vehicles collided like bumper cars.

Officer McNamara got on his feet. He saw another officer aim and poised to fire. "No don't." The officer drew his weapon and fired three rounds at June. They all missed. June lifted his hand, causing the officer to rise several feet in the air. And with the drop of his hand, June let the officer fall. It knocked him out cold.

A helicopter hovered over them, shining a light on June. It hovered for a few minutes before landing several yards away. Additional patrol cars arrived. One tried to run June over, but it stopped two inches away from him and tumbled back with the flick of June's wrist. June rotated his palm and lifted a few street cars, launching them like darts at the police.

"Stop!" a voice cried out.

In the distance stood his mother, Ahnie, next to Dr. Risk.

"Stop this June," Ahnie said.

June felt his energy dwindle at the sight of his mother. He fell to his knees, exhausted.

A man with dark shades rushed in and struck June with a baton-like stick that had two metal prongs protruding from its tip. It sent an electrical shock though June's body, rendering him unconscious.

16

A Global Situation

The steady rhythm of the pulse monitor was the only sound in the room. Elizabeth Risk lay comatose, as she had been since the day she found Charles and Joy together. By her side sat the only man she'd ever loved.

The room was exceptionally large. Not a typical room for patients at CURE. Besides the highly advanced equipment, the decor was comfortable and homey. In fact, Charles made sure this room was an exact replica of their vacation home in Santorini, Greece. It was her favorite place to visit, and she imagined they would eventually settle there once Charles had 'conquered' the world. The walls were a very soft grey, with touches of blue throughout.

The ceiling was painted the same blue as the rooftops of homes on the Grecian island. Charles had his own attachment to the region. It was there that he had an epiphany of what his contribution to mankind would be.

Elizabeth's appearance didn't reflect her current circumstances. Her lips were red, and she was well groomed. Unless he was overseas, Charles visited Elizabeth twice every day. Sometimes he would visit her early before heading into the office hoping to catch her waking up—as if she had been sleeping for one long night.

"Why are you standing there, like you've seen a ghost?" Elizabeth said. She didn't speak the words, but Charles did hear them. "You've been working all night, haven't you?" she said with a smile. The light around her was soft and radiant.

"I'm sorry," Charles said. His lips did move as a tear fell from his eye. He put his head down as he wiped it away. When he looked back up, she was back in bed as she had been for the last year. He walked over and gently stroked her hair.

"See you soon," he said as he exited the room. He said it as if it were true, as if this was one big dream, and she would wake up at any moment.

"I apologize for keeping you waiting, gentlemen," Dr. Risk said as he walked into the boardroom. He brushed the corner of his eye with his thumb and composed himself. Sitting in front of him were distinguished leaders from around the world. Some were present via satellite. Charles walked to the end of the long table.

Each pair of eyes followed him, anxiously awaiting his announcement. On the table was a metallic remote with a single button. He picked it up and pivoted on his heel, pointing it at the wall behind him. A detailed holographic map of the world appeared. As he made an arc motion with his hand, other images trickled in. These were of random people—Black, White, Asian, and European ranging in age from thirteen to thirty.

He spread his fingers out, bringing back the map. He brought his hands together like in a prayer position and spread them apart, splitting the screen in two. On the left was the map; on the right was the gallery of headshots. When the images settled, he turned around to address everyone.

"Good morning, Mr. President, Madame Secretary, Prime Minster, Secretary of Defense, esteemed colleagues, world leaders. You are all seeking answers to the global anomalies that ravaged our lands almost a year ago."

"The earthquake in New York…" Video footage of Manhattan, after it had been decimated populated the screen. It showed dead bodies lying in rubble and a parade of people covered in dust.

"Munich, Germany…" Charles waved his hand toward the console and a montage of images and video of the destruction in Munich slid onto the screen. "Tokyo…" An aerial shot showing pillars of smoke and destruction lit up the screen. "Australia, Prague, Thailand… And even Southern California…"

A sequence of numbers in red text accumulated on the wall as he referenced each city. It stopped at 24,573.

"This is the current number of lives we lost… in just one day."

Everyone in the room uncomfortably re-adjusted themselves in their seats.

"I founded CURE to find solutions to world problems that the collective scientific community had yet to solve—events that your experts cannot explain. Within a short time, our research has led to the cure or advanced treatment of almost all modern illnesses."

On the screen flashed the words CANCER, STDs, and a plethora of other diseases. All had a checkmark and 'CURE' marked next to them. Charles walked around the room, making eye contact with every official as he spoke.

"AIDS, Cancer, the common cold. These are all things of the past thanks to our efforts here at CURE. We've also made monumental advancements in technology: drones that can take out an enemy convoy without risking the safety of our troops, cars that drive themselves, cell phone batteries that last for weeks and recharge in a mere thirty seconds…"

"With all due respect, Doctor. We appreciate and respect your contributions, but we don't need a history lesson," the President interrupted.

Dr. Risk smirked. "Of course not, Mr. President. I merely wanted to remind everyone why you trust us to do what we do. For what I'm about to reveal may be a bit hard to swallow."

He paused and looked around the room. "Let's just say that it requires a type of thinking that not many people have had to employ."

Everyone sat up straighter. Dr. Risk gestured toward the screen, and the headshots of random people illuminated.

"Whatever is happening to our world has not only brought destruction, but it has taken our species to another level."

Everyone looked at each other and back at the doctor with puzzled expressions.

"At CURE we believe there is something more happening in our world than these climatic anomalies. We believe…" He paused. "No, we have proof that the next stage of evolution is upon us."

Murmurs echoed throughout the boardroom. Dr. Risk motioned with his pointer finger, beckoning two of his armed guards. They escorted a beautiful girl with dark hair and green eyes into the room. It was Robyn, dressed in a fitted, white jumpsuit.

"Ladies and gentlemen… meet Robyn." She proudly stood at the end of the table as everyone stared at her. None of the women seemed impressed.

"Is she … a cyborg?" the Prime Minister hesitantly asked.

"No, she is one-hundred-percent human. Flesh and blood."

"Are we missing something, Charles?" the President asked as the others whispered among themselves.

"Robyn, let's show my guests why they are here," said Dr. Risk.

"Yes, Doctor," she responded with a cold smile.

Robyn spread her arms over her head, and the conference room table levitated into the air. Everyone jumped from their seat, except Mr. Carter, the Secretary of Defense.

"I'm not spooked by your parlor tricks Risk," Mr. Carter said. He was a stern man, hard-faced. His coat displayed medals and badges highlighting an impressive career in the Armed Forces.

Robyn pointed her palms toward him and spread her fingers. He clutched his chest as she levitated him over the table.

"Ben, now," Dr. Risk ordered.

The guard at the rear of the room removed his handgun from his holster and fired eight rounds at Mr. Carter, who was still levitating over the table. He covered his face, and everyone scurried.

"Open your eyes, Mr. Carter," Dr. Risk said.

Still hovering in the air, three feet above the table, he cautiously opened his eyes. Eight bullets hovered only inches from his face, suspended in motion.

Dr. Risk turned to Robyn and nodded. The bullets fell to the table like loose change. Robyn lowered her hands, and simultaneously, the table and Mr. Carter lowered to the ground.

"Please, everyone, no need for alarm," said Dr. Risk. "Robyn is one of us. As compliant as any soldier. She won't bring you any harm."

"And how can you be sure of that?" asked the President. "Are there more like her?"

"The answer to your second question, Mr. President, is yes."

Another gasp echoed through the room.

"Unfortunately, we don't know exactly how many of 'her' there are, but we do know she is not the only one."

"And how can you guarantee her cooperation? How do we know that her kind won't turn on us one day?" the President asked.

"'Her kind?'" laughed Dr. Risk. "I believe we are looking at what we will all eventually become." Dr. Risk looked around the room and saw fear in every set of eyes.

"As long as we can get to them before they understand what they're capable of, we can guarantee their cooperation, Mr. President," Dr. Risk said.

"You see, their power comes at a price. And the current structure of the human body is not capable of handling it."

"In English," the President snapped.

"My apologies, Mr. President."

Victoria entered the room with a syringe of purple liquid and injected it into Robyn's arm. "Once they discover their abilities and aggressively use them, without the serum, they have a lifespan of one or two years. Without this serum, developed here at CURE, they die."

"What do you mean by aggressive?" The President asked.

"They are telekinetic. Moving everyday objects, or interacting with our digital interface has no effect. But anything more involved takes a heavy toll on them."

"But how is this connected to the events around the world? Are you saying they are responsible?" the President asked.

Dr. Risk directed their attention to the screen behind him. "These acts are connected, but there's no evidence to suggest that it was done by anyone."

"After what you just showed us, how can there not be cause for concern?"

Dr. Risk exhaled. "Our research indicates these may be... an act of God. We think He's trying to tell us something."

The President exhaled. Everyone else erupted in laughter. Charles angrily smacked the table.

"We're running out of time! Mr. President, I know how insane this sounds! But we..." Charles realized he was shouting at the President of the United States and changed his tone. He waited a beat before completing his statement.

"We have to wrap our heads around the idea that this may be beyond scientific comprehension. And if we don't act now, we may face another incident that may be even worse. Now, we all have families and people we love. That is what drives me every day."

A video feed of his ill wife in her bed appeared on the screen.

"I fear this is only the beginning."

17

CURE: Part 5

"I've been having some crazy dreams too," June said. His voice echoed throughout the cell. "I know it sounds crazy... but I think I may be able to tele..."

Novelle was comforting Miko from her nightmare. Her mood shifted when something caught her attention. She pressed her index finger to her lips, prompting June to stop mid-sentence. The sound of boots approaching their cell was barely audible but it was there. It became louder until a clank released the door. Two guards rushed in. One positioned himself in front of Novelle and June while the other pulled Miko from the bed.

"Leave her alone!" Novelle shouted.

The guard in front of them placed his trigger finger on his

weapon, silencing her. They quickly exited the cell—taking Miko with them.

"At least she's out," June said.

"I don't trust what's going on around here."

"What makes you say that?"

"I just feel it," Novelle said. "I can feel it every day I wake up in this place. I can feel everyone's pain. It comes and goes. But sometimes, it's overwhelming."

June looked at his legs and tried to move them. "I just wished my legs would come back already. Tired of feeling like a loser around here."

"Still not able to feel anything?" Novelle asked.

"When I try to move them, nothing happens," June replied. "It's like my body is fighting to heal itself, but something's blocking it."

"So you're telling me if I do this..." Novelle said as she pinched June's thigh, "You won't feel anything?"

Shockingly, June's leg kicked up in response.

"Oh shit," June said.

"You felt that?"

"Yeah, I actually did. Do it again."

"Ok, you ready?"

"Do it."

Novelle raised her palm as high as she could. June braced for the impact. She swung her hand onto June's leg with more force.

"Did you feel that?" Novelle asked.

June slowly opened his eyes.

"Nope, nothing."

"Damn."

She raised her fist this time, to strike him again, and her

mind jumped to a beach. Instead of being in the cell with June, she found that she was leaning over an injured young man wearing a sports jersey. She could feel the ocean breeze blow through her hair as chaos loomed around her.

"Novelle... Novelle. Hey, you ok?"

She snapped back to the cell, her fist still held high.

"You all right?" June asked.

"Yeah. I just had another vision."

"What did you see?"

"I'm not sure. But I felt something. Hold still."

She placed her hands on June's legs and closed her eyes, trying to go back to the place where her mind recently jumped.

"The visions are coming faster," Novelle said. "Before they were only when I slept. But now it's more random."

"When I saw you on that train, I never thought we'd be locked up together," June said. "So much has happened. Hard to believe this time last year the only thing on my mind was making State. Track was my life. Until the day I saw you."

"But I've never been to Brooklyn," Novelle said.

"I'm telling you, this girl was a spitting image of you," June replied. "Something about her eyes. I mean, your eyes. Not the... well you know what I mean. They're different from when I saw you that day. But the way you looked at me. Something about it. It made me feel like you knew me. Like we'd known each other for a long time. Can't explain it." He turned away, embarrassed. "I'm sorry," he added. "I remember how much I wished my father would have been able to see me run. My mother said he was a track star in college too. Showed me some of his old medals and pictures. That's why I joined the team. I felt it was my only connection to him."

"And now that I can't use my legs at all…"

Novelle's heart melted as she felt his pain. She rubbed his back gently.

"You know, my father was in the military. The last time he deployed, I was only eight. Seemed like forever ago. There I was, this little snot-nosed boy looking up to his dad. Even though I was sad, I knew he was doing a great thing. He said something to me that didn't make sense until recently." June shook his head and placed his finger under his chin. "He saw something in me that even with these gifts I still don't see in myself."

Novelle could sense his pain.

"My father told me that great strength is given to people called to protect those who cannot protect themselves. It can't all be a coincidence, can it? These powers, they have to mean something."

"I can feel the love you have for your father," Novelle said. "You miss him very much."

June turned his face away, worried he may start crying. Novelle sensed his vulnerability and touched his face to assure him it was ok.

"Hey…" she spoke softly. "I'm sure he's proud of you."

Their eyes met, and June felt her energy pulling him in. It felt warm and familiar. He leaned toward her and their lips softly met.

As they kissed, the world around them transitioned to total darkness. A flame mysteriously ignited just a few feet away. Others followed, illuminating a cathedral-sized hall with marble floors. The moment somehow felt familiar. And as he stared into her green eyes, he somehow understood why they were there.

They looked like themselves, but much older. The moment was interrupted by an overwhelmingly cold undercurrent. June jumped back. Novelle didn't want to let him go, but somehow she knew that she had to. He walked down the majestic corridor following the path of flames that led to a large door. As he approached, the door opened, revealing the outside world. They were on a structure perched high on a large rock, somehow floating several hundred feet above ground. June, now dressed in all black, had a golden charm around his neck. It was a ring connected to a tall U shape. He looked toward Earth, which spun slowly below, and saw something— something he knew he had to face.

He stepped forward and leapt off the rock, plunging gracefully. A thunderous boom shook the ground upon his landing. A dark, manly figure, dressed in a long black coat, spoke to him. Its face was liquid metal and devoid of facial features.

"This is forbidden, Netfa," he said to June. The voice had a deep rumble that bounced through the sky.

"I've made my choice Adorie," June replied.

"That is not our right. That is not our purpose. We serve to maintain The Balance."

They walked toward each other with focused intensity. The crash of thunder became more dramatic with every step.

"I will not let you take her," June said.

"She has nothing to do with this."

"She has *everything* to do with this," Adorie sharply replied.

A vein of lightning shot from the sky into Adorie's hand, transforming into a long, mythical sword. June gestured to the sky, summoning an identical weapon.

With blinding speed, Adorie flew into the air and descended upon June, raising his sword to deliver a downward blow. June leapt towards him, countering the attack with his blade. On impact, their weapons ignited into a bright blue flame.

They battled fiercely, flying a thousand feet above the ground, swinging their swords at each other with calculated force. The clash of their weapons sent shockwaves along the desert, causing towering waves of sand. June was amazed at the sheer display of power. He appeared to be equally matched with his enemy.

Adorie began to conjure power with his sword when a white ray of light pierced through the clouds between them. June felt a stream of energy surge through his body preventing him from moving. He struggled as the beam crept toward him, blinding his sight.

The entire scene dissipated as quickly as it had appeared, and June found himself back in the majestic hall with Novelle, his hand hovering over her chest. He could feel her energy being pulled from her body as she reached out. She began to lose her breath, and her heart rate decelerated. Her instincts kicked in, prompting her to push away from June, but her body ignored the commands.

When June finally let go, she fell to the floor, but Novelle found she was no longer present in that body. She saw herself lying dead on the floor even though she was still there standing.

When she turned to the right, there was June, but dressed in white CURE attire as they were in the cell.

"Hey, you ok?" June asked. "Novelle…"

She was back in the cell with June, who was leaning over her. She had somehow blacked out.

"Another vision?" June asked.

Novelle felt disoriented but noticed something was different about June.

"You're standing," she said.

"Yes, I am," June replied. "Yes I am."

18

Dr. Charles Risk

Gradin's designer shoes tapped down the hall as he approached his father's office. He wasn't going to wait. He had something to get off his chest.

"Why do you hate me so much?" Gradin said as he barged into Charles' office. "You care more about this company than your own damn son."

There was a buzzing sound from Charles' phone. It was Lisa.

"That's enough!" shouted Charles. "You're drunk and I have important business to attend to."

"Screw that!" Gradin replied. "I know your meeting with the President didn't go as planned. You know why? Cause you're freakin' nuts! You're crazy if you think anyone's gonna believe that God is trying to warn us."

He stumbled into Charles' desk and snatched the framed picture beside his laptop. The photo was of him, Charles, and Elizabeth.

Charles' phone buzzed again.

"All this shit is fake! All of it," Gradin said as he smashed the frame onto the floor. "You don't care about us at all!" Tears fell from Gradin's face as he looked down at the photo. He brushed a few shards of glass away and picked up the picture. He looked at it for a moment before ripping it in half.

"What are you doing?" Charles asked. His phone buzzed yet again. He reached over and pressed the button to speak.

"What is it, Lisa?"

"Sir, I'm so sorry but I need to speak with—"

"Not now Lisa."

"Sir, it's important."

"Lisa, I said not now."

"But sir, you said…"

Gradin wiped the tears from his eyes. He dropped one half of the picture to the floor. "And now you've lost me too," he said as he stormed out.

Lisa saw it as an opportunity to enter.

"Send someone to clean this up," Charles ordered as Lisa carefully approached the doorway.

"Sir, I'm really sorry."

"My son is a drunk. And, of course, everything's always my fault." He turned around to face the city.

"Sir, there's a situation."

Lisa took a breath. Somewhat confident before, she now seemed hesitant to speak

"Sir, um."

"Out with it, Lisa."

"I'm so sorry, sir. Elizabeth…"

A thought hit Charles and he sprung to the phone.

He pressed a button.

"Raymond, what's the status on Elizabeth?"

"I'm confused, Charles. Gradin said he wanted to tell you personally."

"Tell me what?" Charles barked. He was hunkered over the desk breathing heavily.

Raymond took a breath before responding. "We lost her, Charles. Just a few minutes ago. I'm sorry."

Lisa opened her mouth to speak but caught the words before they escaped.

"Sir?"

Charles sat down in his leather chair, placing his elbows on the desk, his hands draped over his face.

20 years ago

"I'm sorry Charles, but the board has made its decision. It's final. My hands are tied."

A younger Charles Risk sat in an office with Raymond Dreskel, Dean of Harvard.

"They can't do this! I'm the most significant Social Science professor this institution has ever had. This is bullshit, and you know it!"

Raymond dropped a book on the desk. "Mass genocide? Special selection? It might as well have been *Mein Kampf.* This is what you've been teaching our students?" He paused and shook his head. "I get it. You're smart, brilliant in fact, but I can't protect you anymore."

"What I teach, Raymond, is for the good of mankind," Charles replied. "We are the problem. We cause everything! Wars! Famine! The dramatic rise in population has made our world unstable."

Raymond shook his head again as Charles continued his rant.

"Global warming? Pollution? It's all a joke. The only thing hurting this planet is us. But I'm not saying we should take a billion people into a field and slaughter them. We just have to figure a way to slow down population growth and think of a way to cleanse our society."

"Cleanse?" echoed Raymond. "And who gets to choose who goes and who stays?"

"It's simple. Everyone is assigned a task in The System."

Raymond wasn't buying it.

"Not by how much money they make or how many sports cars they drive, but how they can be a contributing member of society," Charles said.

He leaned toward Raymond.

"Life is a gift, a privilege. We've become arrogant. Look at our ecosystem. Everything co-exits harmoniously with the environment, except for us. My theory simply states that if we continue down this path, if we don't change, we're going to end up like the dinosaurs. The genocide you and those pompous assholes are accusing me of will be by our own hand."

"Look, I'm not accusing you of anything, Charles. This is Harvard, not community college. Your curriculum simply is not consistent with our program. It was hard enough to convince the board not to pursue criminal charges."

"On what grounds?"

"The kid that shot up the mess hall was one of your students, Charles. His last words were 'for a clean world,' which, I might add, is a quote from your book."

"I can't be held responsible if some whacko kid misquotes me and goes on a rampage," said Charles, smacking the desk.

"Charles, look at me. I'm your friend. But this cleansing the population theory never sat well with me. I assumed it was a casual idea. Ambitious at best. Maybe you were trying to win a Pulitzer or something. Didn't know you'd already written a book about it under an alias. Then using that book to alter the curriculum? I'm sorry, but the decision is final. To protect both sides, the school has decided to not make this public, pending your immediate resignation."

"Well they better lawyer up. I'm not taking this lying down, Raymond."

"C'mon Charles. You're putting me in a tough spot here. Trust me, it's better to just move on from this. You're young and still have your whole career ahead of you. You don't want this stink following you around."

Raymond stepped out from behind his desk and sat next to Charles.

"Look, I'll write a letter of recommendation to whomever I need to. Just let me know where you're headed. But your time here at Harvard is done. They're giving you a nice severance package. Take the deal Charles, and take Elizabeth somewhere nice."

"Like that place in Greece she always talks about. Enjoy yourself for a while. Maybe even pursue that Med-Tech startup you've always talked about. Resign, take the money and put this behind you."

"Sir?"

"Sir?" Lisa asked. "Is there... is there anything I can do?"

Charles didn't respond immediately. He sat still as he processed the fact that his wife was no longer alive.

19

CURE: Part 6

"These visions, they've been trying to tell me something. And after trying to heal you, I think our visions aligned. I'm not sure, but I may have an idea why all of this is happening. It took a while to piece it together but the same images that are in my visions, are also in yours."

"So why do you think this is happening?" June asked.

Novelle took a deep breath and exhaled through her nose before responding.

"We fell in love."

June's facial expression didn't fully grasp her statement.

"Who's we?"

"I'm not sure. Maybe in a past life. I don't know… sounds crazy but I think that we are the reason for all of this."

"And how did you come to that?"

"Think about it for a moment. In our vision together, you killed me by making my heart stop. But you weren't in control. It was like you were ordered to. Like you had no choice."

"Wait. So killing you is how you think us being together caused us to have powers in the future?"

"That part I'm unsure of. But I know that whatever we were doing displeased someone very powerful. And in an attempt to make it right, you had to take my life. It was like you were being punished for something."

"I'm still trying to swallow the fact that you and I were…"

"Yes, we were in love. It was real. And when I kissed you, I felt everything."

A loud bang against the door startled them.

BOOM! BOOM!

The door slid open, revealing the bruised face of James, one of the nurses.

"Come with me. Right now!"

They scurried down the halls, hiding behind the pillars if they heard any movement.

"What's going on?" Novelle asked.

A few guards ran past them before James could answer.

"We gotta move. If they know you're not in your cell we'll be made," whispered James. He entered a sequence of numbers on the keypad. The loud scrape of the door blew their cover.

"Hey! Stop!" yelled a guard as he dashed toward them.

The trio ran through the doorway as soon as it was wide enough. James activated the sequence on the other side to shut it.

"Dammit, my code's not working." He took a few steps back and rammed the panel with his elbow. It shorted the system, shutting the door.

The guard closest to the door on the other side loaded his weapon and positioned himself to fire.

"Let's go!" James yelled.

The guard fired his weapon, striking the door as it shut. They ran down the hall and turned the corner. James took them through a narrow corridor that led to a laboratory. They paused to catch their breath before entering.

"I've been trying to figure out what was going on around here," James said. "Things just never made sense. Take a look at this." He flicked the lights on to show them the rows of cylinders filled with serum.

"I wanted to believe they were helping you guys, but their methods never made sense. I sent some of the serum to a contact and he came back with some interesting results."

James activated the computer terminal and began showing them pages of documents. "There are inactive ingredients in the serum. Ethanol, scopolamine, and midazolam."

"Isn't that what's in a truth serum?" Novelle asked.

June was shocked Novelle knew what it meant.

"Exactly. But there's more. Some of it I can't make out, but the other substances I know have been used to treat high-functioning psychiatric patients."

"What does it all mean?" June interrupted.

"There has to be a way to trigger the effect. But if it's what I think it is, they have been testing a method to control all the patients."

"Control us? What?" June asked.

"That's what I've been trying to figure out. I did some digging and found this." He typed a complex sequence of numbers on the keyboard that pulled up a chat log.

Victoria Dang, Feb 12, 2015 1:12PM:

Charles, the subjects are responding well to the serum. But there is one anomaly, Novelle Chenoa. Her immune system is unlike the others. There is almost no effect on her cerebral activity even after stronger doses.

Charles Risk, Feb 12, 2015 1:30PM:

Interesting, I wonder what it could mean. Did you try an earlier version of the serum?

Victoria Dang, Feb 12, 2015 1:35PM:

Yes, same result. But I have a theory sir. Based on the tests we ran when she arrived, she seems to have an unusually high stem cell count. The data suggests an abnormality in her bone marrow. To be frank, I think she has the ability to heal. I can't confirm without more tests. But I think we should keep her under strict supervision.

Charles Risk, Feb 12, 2015 2:15PM:

Fascinating! Great work.

Victoria Dang, Feb 12, 2015 2:20PM:

Are we still proceeding as planned?

Charles Risk, Feb 12, 2015 2:21PM:

Yes.

Victoria Dang, Feb 12, 2015 2:25PM:

I have a concern. What if we're wrong? What if there's another way?

Charles Risk, Feb 12, 2015 2:28PM:

This is the only way.

Victoria Dang, Feb 12, 2015 2:29PM:

But millions of people may die. I'm having a hard time with that.

Charles Risk, Feb 12, 2015 2:31PM:

Victoria, this is the only way to truly solve the world's problems.

Charles Risk, Feb 12, 2015 2:32PM:

Phones, apps and curing diseases is a waste.

Charles Risk, Feb 12, 2015 2:33PM:

Earth is dying. Look around you. Why do you think all these disasters have occurred in such a small span of time?

Charles Risk, Feb 12, 2015 2:34PM:

How long before there's nothing left? Yes, people will die. But the planet will be much stronger. Our race will survive.

Charles Risk, Feb 12, 2015 2:36PM:

It is the only way to repair the damage that's already been done.

Charles Risk, Feb 12, 2015 2:37PM:

I need to know you are ok with this. Can the serum guarantee 100% compliance?

Victoria Dang, Feb 12, 2015 2:44PM:
…yes doctor.

A rattle against the door startled them.

"Shit, they've found us."

James pulled a cell phone from his back pocket and made a call. "This is agent James Cooper. I've secured two assets. Need immediate evac." He paused for a moment to look over at June and Novelle. "I've been made," he said.

June and Novelle stood frozen.

"Wait, so you're what, an FBI agent?" Novelle snapped.

A bang that sounded like metal on metal shook the room.

"This way," James prompted.

"We're not going anywhere with you," responded Novelle.

"Please, there's no time to explain. If you come with me, I can protect you," James said.

"You gotta clear something up for me," Novelle asked. "What do the FBI want with Risk, unless you already know he's planning something?"

James exhaled. "Listen, a few weeks ago, Risk told the US Government about your kind and all the things you're capable of. Let's just say they felt more comfortable keeping a closer eye on things moving forward."

"So let me guess, they wanna use us as weapons now?" June asked.

James ignored his comment. "I was placed as a precautionary measure. Dr. Risk and CURE have always done right by us. But this… this is something else."

"So are you really a nurse? Or just a spy?" Novelle asked.

"Look, I had no idea what I was getting into. Even when I read the report I still didn't believe it. But trust me, I'm not your enemy."

The door burst open and several guards rushed in. Behind them was Robyn.

"Find them, now!" she ordered.

The guards searched the immediate area of the lab. They didn't find anything there, leading them towards the large secondary room.

"Shit, they're gonna find us," Novelle said.

"There's an emergency exit this way. Hurry," James warned.

They ran toward a door on the east end of the room.

A guard saw Novelle. "I've got 'em! Over here!"

James rushed him from the side and knocked him out with two punches. Before he could turn around, another guard had a gun pressed against his head.

"Not so fast."

Robyn approached as the other guards held him down.

"You're never gonna get away with this," James said. He struggled as the guards restrained him.

Robyn smirked and signaled to the other guards. "Find the others. Bring them to the control room."

Novelle and June ran up a staircase. A guard was on his way down. June raised his hand and swung it left. The guard flew to the side and hit his head against the wall. They made it several stories up to a door that led to the ground floor. Novelle turned the handle, but it wouldn't open, even after she threw her shoulder into it. "It's either locked or stuck."

"Nothing's ever locked," June said.

He hovered his hand over the handle and attempted to move it with telekinesis.

"Shit, it's not working."

"You can't just wave your hand over something and have it magically open it. You have to move what's needed, or just break it."

Behind them, several guards were approaching from the lower levels. June pulled his hand back and thrust it forward, denting the door. He repeated the motion two times, and the door swung open. An alarm went off. Oddly, the lobby was completely empty.

"We gotta warn the others."

June paused, looking toward the entrance, while Novelle sprinted for the elevator. She turned back to June when she realized he wasn't following her.

"What are you doing? We don't have much time," she said.

"I gotta see my mom. She needs me."

"Don't you understand what's going on? If we don't stop them, a lot of people are going to lose their mothers," Novelle said.

"Hey! You! Stop!" yelled one of the guards. Several others rushed through the broken door. Two of them fired a dart from a special handgun that struck June in the neck. June raised his hand but found his strength was gone. He struggled to turn his head as he lost control of his body. With his remaining strength, he pushed several guards away with telekinesis. Another dart came from behind him, and he fell to the ground. One of guards pressed his knee into June's back and restrained his hands. As June began to black out, he saw Novelle get taken into custody.

"Leave her alone!" June yelled. "Leave… her…alone…"

20

CURE: Part 7

"Choose," said a deep, familiar voice.

June opened his eyes to find himself in a modern, white room with a large horizontal window. Through the glass was a view of Earth from outer space. Next to the window stood a man with his back turned toward June.

"Where am I?"

The man spoke, but his mouth did not move.

"Home."

June was confused. "Home?" he asked.

The man waved his hand. In the window was June's mother in her living room. It felt as if they were there with her. As if he could reach out and touch her.

Ahnie's room began to shake violently. It tilted, causing her to slide towards the far wall and hit her head. She lay unconscious as the ground continued to rumble.

"Mom! What is happening?" June frantically asked.

The man waved his hand again, and now in the window was Novelle, floating mid-air with her arms outstretched. She was unconscious but breathing. Just then, a fire sparked around her. Her eyes opened as the flames grew stronger.

"Help!" she screamed. "Help me June."

June tried to approach the window. He stepped forward but didn't seem to be getting any closer.

"Help!" Novelle screamed. "June, help me!"

He took several more steps, but the window was still the same distance away. Frustrated, he started to run, but the man and the window now seemed even further away.

"Why? Why are you doing this?" June cried.

"Soon, you will choose," the man said.

Tears fell from June's eyes as the flames completely engulfed Novelle. He turned his face away as she screamed in agonizing pain. He felt his anger building. He took another step forward, and again the window and man zoomed further away. The sound of Novelle suffering was too much for him. His legs gave way, and he fell to his knees.

"No, please. Don't do this. Please."

A surge of energy rushed through his body. He reached toward the window and focused on Novelle. The smell of her hair and skin touched his nose. He closed his eyes and imagined that she was standing there, right in front of him.

A tear rolled down his cheek as he extended his hand in front of him. He opened his eyes and felt his body move through the space. The window was much closer now. He closed his eyes and focused again.

When he opened them, he was restrained to a chair with a guard on each side. It was a room at CURE he had never been in before. In front of him was a colossal multi-panel display. Seated in front of it was Dr. Charles Risk. On the screens played video feeds from around the globe. From the busy streets of Times Square to the green hills of Ireland. As he struggled, he felt an injection pierce both arms. The initial sting was painful, but his reaction to the injection was something he had become accustomed to.

"Sorry about that. But we can't risk you doing something you may regret," said Dr. Risk. "You're being injected with a modified serum every three minutes. Call it an insurance policy, to keep things civil."

He gestured towards the guards. Novelle and James were pushed into the room by two additional guards. Robyn was directly behind them.

"I believe in second chances," said Dr. Risk. "Which is why you're still here. Unfortunately, it's not a courtesy I extend to everyone."

At that moment Robyn placed her hands over James' neck, hovering just two inches away from it. He began to levitate, struggling against the pressure. She spread her fingers apart and quickly clasped them into a fist. James collapsed to the ground.

"No!" Novelle screamed.

"You are a fascinating one, June. What is it that makes you different?" Charles asked. "All that power. Yet, a simple injection can take it all away."

The door to the adjacent chamber opened, and all the patients filed in like soldiers. Among them was Miko. Their eyes had all changed to a gray color, dulled from their usual green. Except for Terrence.

Terrence walked to June and crouched before him.

"How's it hanging man?" June looked up to find Terrence's arrogant smirk.

"You know when I saw you the first time, I expected someone bigger, not the little shit you turned out to be."

"Really." June replied.

"I know about your little incident with your buddy. What was his name? Ah, that's right… Jonas. What a loser."

June violently jerked in his restraints.

Dr. Risk approached, placing his hand on Terrence's shoulder like a proud dad would to his son.

"Terrence is how I was able to find you. All of you."

June and Novelle watched in shock as Terrence removed the green contacts from his eyes.

"So you're not one of us after all," Novelle said.

"Sorry to disappoint you sweetheart," Terrence replied. He sauntered over to Novelle and grabbed under her chin. "But if you're nice, maybe we can work something out."

She lunged at him, but the guards held her back.

"Let's go. Right now. Me and you. I'll show you just how nice I can be," she said.

"Terrence is a medium," said Dr. Risk. "After we found you on the beach, we were curious. Given that you were positioned at the disaster's main point of impact, we were curious how you survived. Once we realized how different you were, it didn't take us long to find the others."

"So that's why you never used your powers," June said.

"And here you were thinking it was my Boy Scout honor that held me back," Terrence laughed.

"Terrence's gift has made many things possible," Dr. Risk said.

"That's your secret. That's how you've been able to stay ahead of everyone," Novelle said. "You've been using a psychic."

"Perceptive," Dr. Risk said. "Terrence is a descendant of the Ganzfeld experiments and has been very useful all these years. Which is why this isn't easy for me."

Dr. Risk made eye contact with one of the guards, who removed a firearm from his waistband and fired a shot into Terrence's chest. He flew back from the impact of the bullet, hitting the polished marble floor.

A buzzer signaled the opening of metal doors, revealing a view of the city's west end. The bright sun scorched everyone's eyes. A guard placed another chair directly in front of June. Dr. Risk positioned himself in the chair, barely a foot away from his captive. June lifted his head and locked eyes with the doctor.

"You're a monster," he scowled.

"Hm," laughed Dr. Risk. "I'm sure many others share your point of view. But once the dust has settled and tears have dried, the world will thank me for saving them." He pushed himself back and stood above June. "This is the revival of our species we have all been waiting for."

"You can't honestly believe good can come from killing thousands of innocent people," June said. "You're insane."

"Oh, I don't. That's why millions have to die. For there to be change, the act must be significant," said Dr. Risk. "But I think your concern is a bit more... singular?"

Dr. Risk threw his hand back at the grid of screens. At the bottom was a video feed into June's home. His mother went about her daily routine, unaware she was being watched.

"So what is it? What is it that makes you different from the others? Tell me your secret," Charles asked.

"Even if I knew, I would never tell you," June replied.

At that point, a guard held Novelle's arms behind her back while another injected her with serum. Robyn walked over and opened her palm. A second later, another guard removed a handgun from his holster and placed it in her hand. She cocked back the weapon and pointed it between Novelle's eyes.

Dr. Risk responded to the sound of the gun. "See, I happen to know that your girlfriend has an ace up her sleeve. But unlike you, she's not much of a fighter. I ask you again, what is your secret?"

"Don't tell him shit!" yelled Novelle. Her eyes were locked onto Robyn's as she jerked away from the guard's grasp. Robyn slapped the butt of the gun across Novelle's face. She fell to the ground, her head buzzing from the pain.

Victoria entered the chamber holding a digital tablet. On the screen were thumbnail images of each patient with their vitals. She handed it to Dr. Risk.

"Perfect." He entered a sequence of commands into the tablet, causing all the patients to raise their hands toward the city. In the distance was the George Washington Bridge.

"Don't do this, please. There has to be another way. Your mission is to help people. When did life become so meaningless?" pleaded June.

Dr. Risk turned to address him.

"My mission has always been to save the world. I never said anything about saving people."

The monitors switched to display several angles of the George Washington Bridge. A semi and other vehicles suddenly lost control and crashed into the bridge's support, preventing any traffic from entering or exiting the bridge. There was a deep rumble as metal and stone rattled through the structure. The lower deck rocked back and forth. The creak of bending metal could be heard from miles away as the foundation began to shift.

"Stop! Please!" Novelle screamed. "Miko! Don't do this! I know you can hear me. Fight!"

Robyn kicked Novelle in the stomach, sending her sliding across the floor. Novelle looked up in excruciating pain and caught a glimpse of the snow falling outside. She closed her eyes as her mind slipped back.

Flight 3720
One Year Ago

"Ladies and gentlemen, this is your captain speaking. There is unusual turbulence ahead. Please return to your seats and fasten your seat belts."

In the emergency exit row was a middle-aged man with grey streaks in his hair and a kid wearing a gold basketball uniform. Novelle's headphones prevented her from hearing the captain's announcement.

Moments later, the plane shook, and oxygen masks dropped from the ceiling. Everyone was tossed about, like patrons on a roller coaster as the plane battled the turbulence. Novelle reached for her mask, placing it over her mouth. The plane veered to the left, causing some of the upper bins to open. Luggage was tossed around the cabin as the plane spun out of control. It felt like something struck the plane, creating a hole near the rear. Novelle looked out of the window and saw the plane approaching a beach. The tail end of the aircraft started to tear away, and passengers found themselves exposed to the open air.

As she braced for impact, Novelle's mind time-jumped to her waking up on the beach with snow accumulating around her. Then again, her mind jumped to the moment she delivered the blow that resuscitated Michael, Rose's son.

The roar of the tidal wave soon dwarfed the blond toddler's cries. Novelle felt ocean spray against her face as the colossal wave approached. Rose looked up in horror as snow landed on her cheeks. She covered the toddler, turning her back toward the wave.

Novelle crossed her arms, anticipating the impact of the water. A spark ignited within her, making its way through her appendages. A brilliant white light burst from her palm, forming a translucent sphere around her body. Instead of feeling the crushing force of the wave, the water parted around her.

Novelle looked up to find Robyn standing over her in the control room. She raised her leg to deliver another kick. Instinctively, Novelle raised her hand, forming a barrier between her and Robyn. The force field deflected Robyn's attack and sent her stumbling back.

Dr. Risk tapped Miko's image on the tablet, causing her to leave the group and approach Novelle. Robyn planted her feet firmly, conjuring all her power. The force pushed Novelle back, slamming her against the rear wall. Her force field dissipated.

The rage inside June began to grow. He started to hyperventilate as his eyes got brighter. Robyn pivoted, refocusing her telekinesis around June's neck. The serum's effect hadn't worn off, which meant his powers hadn't fully returned. The pressure around his neck grew tighter and tighter.

Novelle recovered from the blow and started crawling toward them. A guard tried to restrain her, but she sent him flying back with telekinesis. She made her way onto her feet and limped toward June. Two guards took aim, firing darts at her. She took control of the darts' trajectory and sent them back at the guards. Robyn repositioned herself between June and Novelle, using her power to keep them apart.

Novelle reached out, knowing that if she could use her healing ability to rid June of the serum's effect, they may have a chance to escape.

Robyn's eyes glowed brighter as she used every ounce of her power. Her eyes transformed from green to red as she pushed her limits. Novelle felt herself being pushed back; Robyn was just too strong. Blood began to drip from her nose as she used all the strength she had. She stretched her hands out, expanding the force field. Their fingertips were now inches apart.

21

CURE: Part 8

Helicopters surrounded the bridge as people scrambled from their vehicles. It began to sway and crackle, and the foundation crumbled beneath the water's surface.

Citizens watched in horror as the news chopper showed a bird's-eye view of the tragic situation.

"It's complete pandemonium as the George Washington Bridge appears to be undergoing some form of collapse. Coast Guard is en route. Let's hope and pray there is a positive outcome here," said the news reporter.

Blood continued to stream from Novelle's nose as she pushed her force field to the limits. If she could just achieve physical contact with June... if she could just reach him...

Terrence, unnoticed and severely wounded, began to crawl slowly toward Robyn. He made his way across the floor until he was within a breath of her. With his last bit of strength he grabbed Robyn, catching her off guard and pulled her to the floor.

The momentary distraction allowed Novelle to make contact with June. A spark ignited between them creating a force that propelled Robyn a few feet away.

Novelle positioned herself in front of June. A surge of energy shot through her core. She focused her mind and released the energy through her hands.

June's eyes flickered as he felt an immense power within him. He broke free of his restraints. As the energy flowed, his body radiated a white light that expanded through the corridor.

The light burst and settled, revealing June levitating in mid-air. His eyes were closed as he softly descended. He opened his eyes, calm and focused.

Dr. Risk hit a few keys on the tablet, commanding all of the patients to direct their powers at June. In unison, they raised their hands toward June and sent a blow in his direction. He crossed his hands and effortlessly deflected the attack. The kickback sent Robyn stumbling into Dr. Risk. The tablet flew from his hand and shattered as it hit the ground.

"Miko!" yelled Novelle.

Miko's eyes flickered between gray and green as she fought the effect of the serum's control. Dr. Risk, realizing June's power was beyond his control, signaled the guards. They filed in and began escorting the patients from the room.

Robyn was back on her feet. Her eyes were glowing red as she summoned her full power. She flew toward June with blinding speed and emitted a blow that pushed him through the back wall. She didn't let up, landing on top of him in mid air and delivering a volley of blows to his face and abdomen.

All the patients were being led down the corridor—still under the serum's trance. Novelle, exhausted, found an ounce of strength to get to her feet.

"Miko!" she yelled again as Miko was being led away. Miko's eyes dissolved to green as she looked around, startled by her surroundings. Novelle reached toward her but found she had no power left. She needed more time to heal.

Robyn came flying back to confront Novelle.

"Didn't forget about you love," she taunted.

June crawled through the hole and called to Robyn.

"Is that all you got?

There was blood oozing from the side of his mouth. He wiped it away with his hand and looked at it. He then tasted it, and gestured at Robyn to come at him, like Bruce Lee would do.

Robyn lunged towards June. Before she reached him, she felt an outside force throw her off. She turned to see it was Miko.

"You little bitch!" Robyn raged, as she turned her attack on Miko. June jumped and spun around in the air, building momentum. He projected a force toward Robyn. She deflected the attack, allowing Miko to retreat toward Novelle.

"Fine, I'll take on all of you."

Robyn planted her feet again, and began conjuring up more power.

Just outside the window, a military-style helicopter appeared on the balcony. When Robyn noticed the aircraft, her eyes morphed back to green. She calmly walked toward the chopper, but stopped to look at June. "Next time, we'll finish this," she threatened.

The door to the copter slid open, unveiling Dr. Risk and the patients. Robyn flew out, landing inside the aircraft as it began to pull away.

June sprinted toward the opening, gaining power as he ran. Just as he reached the window, Novelle called out to him.

"Let her go!"

He stopped.

Novelle appeared badly wounded as she held her abdomen. Miko stood beside her. It hurt June to see Novelle like this.

"We gotta get you some help," he said.

"I'll be fine," she replied. "I just need time to heal."

June's eyes caught Terrence lying dead on the floor, then turned his attention to the monitors. They all had red dots over major parts of the world.

"We can't let them get away. He's going to kill people in every major city."

"The bridge," Novelle exerted. "We gotta help those people."

June looked out the window. The bridge was on the verge of total collapse. "I won't reach them in time," he said. "And even if I do, I don't know if I'm strong enough."

Novelle limped over and gently placed her hand on June's face.

"You can. And you are," she said.

He knew what she meant, but he still doubted if it was real.

"I felt it the first time I saw you. I knew you were special, and capable of doing incredible things. But you have to believe in yourself June. It's the only way."

June looked out, hearing the cries of the innocent people that would soon lose their lives. He slowly walked to the edge of the window and extended his right hand toward the bridge, several miles away. The strong wind at that elevation carried the scent of the Hudson throughout the chamber. His iris jumped left and right as he scanned the bridge, looking for an object to focus on.

There in the distance was a bright blue car that stood out from the rest. He took a deep breath and imagined being there, right next to it. His eyes began to glow as he felt a surge of energy within him. The room pulled away from him. It brought a sense of déjà vu. *Yes, this is what happened the day I reached for the cooler,* he thought. He could smell the motor oil and exhaust smoke from the bridge as he felt his body pull away.

A feeling of amazement washed over him.

It wasn't a hallucination.

He wasn't dreaming.

June, was teleporting.

22

Gemini

What was really a matter of an instant felt much longer to June. Time seemed to decelerate as he reached the bridge. But unlike anyone else, he didn't arrive by car, bus, or foot. The prescribed laws of physics didn't apply here. June had traveled a distance of several miles in a flash, and now he was going to see just how far he could push his limits.

The chaotic noise of people screaming for their lives, crackling metal and tumbling debris rushed his earlobes. But the moment the bottom of his feet felt the rumble of the bridge, a powerful force jerked him backwards into the sky.

The inertia gave him symptoms of vertigo as he was whisked away into the clouds. The bridge was getting smaller and smaller until it was a speck in a sea of blue. Above him, a face and the radiant light of the sun grew stronger until it was too harsh to see.

And again, he heard the voice.

"Choose," it said.

With his eyes closed, June responded.

"What do you want from me?"

"To maintain The Balance," said the voice.

"I don't understand," June replied.

June opened his eyes and around him was the vast emptiness of space. He could see the earth, moon and surrounding stars. A monstrous metallic face eerily emerged from the darkness. It reflected the celestial environment.

"You must choose," it said.

Two portals appeared before June. To his left, the scene of the collapsing bridge, while the other depicted the moments before Jonas was shot by police.

"Jonas," he exhaled.

"You must choose!" demanded the face.

"I can't," June announced. "This. This isn't real…" *Jonas is gone*, he reminded himself.

The images through the portal were so vivid, so undeniable. *What if he was given a second chance to save Jonas? Should he not take it? Yes, for sure this time, he could save him. He would save his best friend.*

He reached towards it and felt the rumble of the bridge from the other portal.

"But all those people. So innocent. They don't deserve to die. I can't let Risk get away with this. I have to do what I can to save them."

"Choose!" the face angrily demanded.

Its eyes started to glow, erupting into a shower of light. The blackness was swallowed whole by it, and again June was in the white space that had plagued his recent dreams.

"Please, I don't know what I'm supposed to do," June pleaded.

A large hooded man appeared and swiftly seized June by his neck. June struggled, using all of his power to tear the hands away. The hands got tighter and tighter. The hood from the man dropped, exposing its face. It was a dark skinned man with chiseled features. And when his eyes locked with June's, he let him go.

June was on his knees, gasping for air. The man stood above him and extended his hand. June reluctantly reached for it and was pulled to his feet.

"You have chosen," the man said.

"I don't understand," June replied.

The man turned his back towards June and extended his hands. A wide horizontal window appeared, and in it was a beautiful vision of Novelle.

"But you have," he assured. "And now, The Balance can be restored."

"It was you. All this time… in my head," June said. "Since the accident."

"I am Adorie. One of two created to maintain this world. Within you lies the spirit of my brother, Netfa."

"Net-fa," June reiterated. "That's what Novelle called me in our vision."

195

Adorie turned towards June, without moving a muscle in his body.

"You choose her."

"Her?"

"When given a choice… your mind, was always led by indecision. Diffidence is a disease that plagues your kind. Yet, when your life was threatened, you did not aspire to save yourself. Instead, your concern was external. Care for another when in an arduous state is not a value found among your kind. It proves you are the one to succeed the role of Netfa."

June looked towards the window and saw the beautiful image of Novelle. He felt her radiance in the room and it gave him strength.

"Now it is time to face your destiny, and restore The Balance," Adorie said.

"But, I still don't understand. What does all of this mean?" Adorie rose his hand towards the window. The image flickered and transitioned to a view of earth from space. The moon positioned itself between the earth and sun, causing an eclipse. But something seemed strange. Thousands of micro beams shot from the earth's surface, headed for the eclipse. The glare subsided, exposing a metallic ring that encircled the globe.

"That phenomenon is The Analog. It predates your world, exposing itself during solar events. But it can only be seen by The Living at the moment of death. You see June, life doesn't end after death. When your body and spirit part, The Soul returns to The Analog, for Judgement."

"This system, designed by The Creator, is The Balance."

"So does that mean I died?" June asked.

"Far from it," Adorie replied.

The window in the white space expanded, and within it displayed the magnificent spectrum of the galaxy.

"I am one of two Gemini, spawned by The Creator. Using two of the brightest stars in *this* universe, he breathed vitality into our forms, simultaneously giving us life and purpose. We are identical in form and power, but separated by duty. Our existence serves to ensure the harmonious function of The Analog. Failure to maintain The Balance would trigger a catastrophic event that would lead your world to its doom."

"So this Creator... made you and your brother... The Gemini. And both of you were given instructions to maintain The Balance?" June asked. "What does it have to do with me and Novelle?"

The window blurred into a brilliant blue color and when it came back into focus, it was a vision of June when he won his first track meet. His teammates cheered him on as he stepped onto the podium to receive the gold medal. It brought a joyful sense of nostalgia to June.

"That feeling you have inside of you right now, is because of me. Happiness, pleasure, forgiveness, love. They are my doing. Know me as the Angel of Life."

"If you are the Angel of Life, then your brother must have been..."

"Yes, until he met her."

The room started to shift, as if the eternal lights were being dimmed, until it was pitch dark. Frail demons with granite skin emerged from beneath the floor, pulling June to the ground. One of them wielded a sharp machete. It taunted June, running the dull end of the blade against June's neck. Several other creatures held June down, while another two held his head forward. The machete demon raised the weapon over its head, ready to strike at June's neck.

"No!" June yelled.

He tried to use telekinesis to no avail.

"Don't. Please. Don't," he cried. He clenched his eyes as tight as he could, trying to envision some other place.

He felt the light touch his eyelids and he re-opened them to see that he was back in the white space, and the demons had vanished.

"Pain, suffering, hate, death. That was Netfa's vocation. But it was too much for him."

"He began to feel for The Living, making it more difficult to perform his duty as a Gemini. Eventually, he fell in love with a woman. Her name, was Layo."

"Layo," June said. "That was Novelle's name in our vision."

"Netfa failed to maintain his side of The Balance. His love for Layo ruined what The Creator had built. And for that, he paid the ultimate price."

The window in the space once again began to change, and in it was the image of a cabin. June walked towards it and found he could reach into the vision. He stepped through the window and found himself physically standing outside the cabin. The sound of the ocean waves gently crashed against the shore, providing a serene ambience. June approached the cabin window and saw a man and woman inside.

She was a beautiful, slender woman with olive skin and piercing green eyes. The man was handsome and muscular, but had a gentleness to him. He lovingly brushed the dark hair away from the woman's face, stroking her cheek with his right hand. The sound of thunder distracted their moment as the strong winds built up, causing a tapping motion at the door.

Outside, a tall figure stood a few yards east of the cabin. It was dressed in a long black coat with a high collar that concealed the bottom half of its face. Its eyes, black as the night.

Inside, the man stood up. He was wearing a similar coat to the figure outside. He slowly made his way to the front door, looking back as if he would be walking out that door for the last time.

The door opened without him touching it and closed behind him the same way. As he stepped forward, the moonlight illuminated his face as his eyes turned black as well.

June followed the man as he stepped away from the cabin, until he was within a few yards of the dark entity.

"You know this is forbidden, Netfa," announced the mysterious figure.

"I've made my choice Adorie," he replied.

"That is not our right. That is not our purpose. We serve to maintain The Balance," Adorie angrily said.

They walked towards each other with focused intensity. The clash of thunder getting more aggressive with every step.

"I will not let you take her from me," Netfa said.

A vein of lightning shot from the sky into Netfa's hand transforming into a long mythical sword. Both of their faces were now covered by dark, angelic masks. Their eyes, still circular abysses of black.

With blinding speed, Adorie flew into the air and descended upon Netfa, raising his sword to deliver a downward blow. Netfa dashed towards him, countering the attack with his blade. Their weapons ignited into a bright blue flame on impact.

While flying almost a half-mile above the ground, they battled fiercely, swinging their swords with calculating force. It was clear the two were equally matched. They moved through the sky, changing direction and speed in a way that defied modern physics.

The clouds above them began to slowly part, revealing a brilliant white ray of light. It shot straight down, blinding Netfa.

Without hesitation, Adorie fell to his knees and bowed his head. The radiance of the beam touched everything within a half mile, but focused solely on Netfa. And as suddenly as it came, the light was gone, reverting the area to its nocturnal state.

Netfa and Adorie rose to their feet in sync. Their weapons dissipated into thin air. The masks morphed into grains of sand, revealing identical faces. Neither of them spoke. Netfa turned his back towards Adorie and headed to the cabin. June followed him.

The cabin door creaked open. Standing there, with his back to the night sky, was Netfa. The mask was gone, completely exposing his face to the light inside.

Layo sprang from the bed, throwing her arms around him. He stood there emotionless with his hands firmly at his side.

A single tear rolled down her cheek and dropped onto the cabin floor. She reached out and grabbed his face while staring into his eyes. They were solid white.

Netfa grabbed her right arm firmly, squeezing so hard it left an impression. She tried to pull away, but her body was unresponsive. All sensation was still there, but she couldn't move.

Netfa raised his right hand slowly over her chest with his fingers spread, as if feeling for something. His other hand still gripping her arm. A sharp pain ran through her body, traveling from her spine to her heart. She began to lose her breath as her heart rate began to decelerate. Her legs ignored her commands as did every other muscle in her body. Her eyes were the only thing she had control over. And as she closed them, the pain grew stronger.

When Netfa finally let go, she collapsed. His iris returned as his demeanor seemed to change. Netfa fell to his knees, frantic of what he had just done. Layo's skin was now as cold as the cabin floor. Devastated, he called out for his brother.

"Adorie!"

Within an instant, Adorie was within the cabin.

"Adorie, you are the giver of life! Save her."

Adorie looked upon the anguish of his brother with cold eyes. Netfa continued to plea until tears began to stream from his eyes. Adorie stood back astonished, but spoke only four words.

"Balance, must be maintained."

Netfa rose to his feet and summoned his ethereal blade. He catapulted out of the cabin, flying towards the sky. Just beyond the clouds, he stopped to contemplate his actions.

As he hovered a thousand feet above ground, he made a decision. With both hands firmly on the weapon, he charged it with power and hurled it further above him, beyond the atmosphere. It climbed several thousand feet until it lost momentum, and started to tumble back down.

Netfa positioned himself in the blade's trajectory as it made its descent back into the earth. He let himself fall and created a forcefield around himself as Adorie flew up to intercept him.

"Netfa, this is madness! Don't destroy this entire world because of one," Adorie said.

"It's already done..." Netfa snapped "This world is already cursed! There is no System. The Analog is corrupt!"

"The Creator has forgiven your transgression," Adorie said. "It is not too late."

He tried to break the field but it was too strong. The blade's velocity increased as it headed straight for Netfa.

"He made me do it," Netfa wept. "He made me kill the one thing I ever loved."

"Because you are death, brother. A fatal lesson. But you knew it would come to this. The Creator can never be challenged."

Netfa released a sporadic burst of energy that increased the mystic shield around him.

"Then let this world come to an end, for I no longer serve The Creator," he said.

Netfa's body crashed into the mountainside, forming a crater half a mile wide, with him in the center. The blade descended upon his skull, shattering his body into a thousand shards of light.

The pockets of light shot into the sky and scattered into several directions. The ground began to rumble violently and at that moment, June felt a blazing sensation in his body. It was an overwhelming sense of power, beyond what he'd felt before. He was then brought back to the white expanse.

Through the window was still a view of earth from outer space. He saw The Analog stutter, but continue to rotate around the globe.

"What is happening?" June asked.

"Netfa's deed has brought harm to The Balance. The Analog is losing momentum, resulting in elemental strife on your planet. Soon, everyone you know and love will die, and your entire world will collapse into the void."

June began hyperventilating, overwhelmed by what he just heard.

"Others that possess the spirit of Netfa must be destroyed so that his Soul can return to The Analog. Once you complete this task, take his place by my side as the other Gemini."

"No, I can't," June sobbed. "I can't be your Angel of Death."

June felt a sourness in his stomach as he contemplated the burden that was upon him. Did he have the capacity to harm Novelle, Miko or any of the others from CURE? And if he could not, would he be able to live knowing it would bring the end to all life on earth? His fear and uncertainty compounded as his thoughts drifted to his mother.

All his life, when faced with an obstacle, she always believed in him. No matter the situation, or how many times he messed up before, she never questioned his potential. *But why*, he thought. *Why did she always believe in me?*

And it was the same with Jonas, and Novelle. Jonas lost his life to save him and Novelle gave up her power to free him.

"I can't let them down," he said under his breath. "All my life people have believed in me. Now I have to believe in myself. If I'm destined to be a Gemini, and they were created equal, then I must be as powerful as Adorie."

June focused on the flame that burned within him. It ignited a brilliant stream of light that shot through his eyes and mouth. Netfa stood back, impressed by June's display of power. June's entire body erupted into a brilliant glow that rivaled the intensity of the sun. The aurora lasted a moment, then subsided, revealing June, reborn. He turned his back towards Netfa and began to walk away.

"What are you going to do?" Netfa asked.

"I will accept my destiny, but not your terms. I will not be your Angel of Death," June replied.

"Do not temper with forces beyond your feeble mind, boy. This is the Law of Existence and it will be enforced! You cannot simply change what The Creator has put forth. Know your place! You are only a man."

June continued his pace. There was a deep crackle as a portal revealed an aerial view of New York City.

"You are right. As a man, I cannot change what was done. But I am no longer just a man."

"I am June. June Gemini."

JUNE GEMINI

To be continued...

ABOUT THE AUTHOR

KOFA is a multi-disciplined creative with a passion for visual storytelling. Based in Los Angeles, he freelances as a director & cinematographer.

JUNE GEMINI is his first novel, which he aims to bring to the digital and silver screen.

More information about Kofa and other works can be found on his website at **www.kofa.tv**.

Connect via **@misterkofa** on all respective social media platforms.